Across A Crowded Room

Praise for Across A Crowded Room, 1st edition

2019 Rainbow Award Honorable Mention for Lesbian Historical

"An engaging romance from the get-go with vivid imagery. Skillfully written and evocative."
-Rainbow Awards

"Great detail and description of the era. Romantic scenes done well. Tastefully erotic."
-Amazon

"The story came alive through the detailed descriptions and you couldn't help but root for Bennie."
-Goodreads

Also by Jane Alden

Evil's Echo

The Payback Murders

Jobyna's Blues (2019 Lesfic Bard Award Winner for Fiction)

A Cass and Ari Adventure Series

The Crystal's Curse (2021 GCLS Goldie Award Winner for Mystery/Thriller)

The Queen's Eye (2024 Lesfic Bard Award Winner for Mystery)

Across A Crowded Room

Jane Alden

Desert Palm Press

Author's Notes

Across A Crowded Room was originally published in 2018. In the first edition, the story ended with Bennie Grant making a difficult decision to leave a loveless marriage, though it meant losing custody of her only child. Her new love, Laura, and she walked away into the sunset with the tentative hope for a happy future together.

The finale left questions: Would Bennie's dream of success as a Broadway director come true? Would Laura be happy leaving her convenient closeted marriage? How would Bennie sustain a relationship with her daughter given a controlling ex-husband and meddling ex-mother-in-law?

Bennie and Laura kept whispering in my ear. They wanted the rest of their story told. Here it is.

Acknowledgements

Jodi Zeramby, publisher of Desert Palm Press, one of the imprints for Penlight Industries, and Lee Fitzsimmons, retired publisher of Desert Palm Press, have been dear, supportive friends from the beginning. I so appreciate their supporting this second edition of *Across A Crowded Room*.

Dedication

To Frances. From that first glimpse till forever. Always in my heart.

Chapter One

Christmas, 1950

Bennie thought it was a bad idea, but Alice insisted that a pre-Christmas cocktail party would be just the right thing to cheer her best friend up. They sped down the road with the top down on Alice's big Packard, even in the frigid air of December.

Alice reached across the leather seat and took Bennie's hand. "I'm worried about you. A distraction getting you out of that cramped, sad little room you insist on living in will do you good." Alice spoke with conviction, but she glanced over, looking for affirmation. "I promise we'll leave whenever you like."

"I know you and parties." Bennie squeezed Alice's hand. "You're such a good friend to worry about me, but I'm afraid this is something I have to go through. No way to make it better. And for your information, I'm not living in a cramped, sad little room. I'm teaching drama in a fine girls' boarding school and enjoying it. I love seeing the girls discover their talents. I don't know what I'd do without it, in fact, being away from Livie at Christmas. And directing at the community theater fills up the rest of my time."

They rode in silence for a while. Alice turned down the volume on the radio. "Do you mind if I ask about the separation? Are you and Will any closer to a resolution?"

"No. We meet next week in his lawyer's office for another session of what Will calls 'pre-divorce planning.' He was so anxious, after our big blowup, to throw me out of our home and take Livie to live at his mother's. Now I think he's using this time to make me come to my senses as he would put it and side-line the divorce."

"Has he sold the house yet?"

"No, and that's another sign that he's hoping for a reconciliation. It's sitting empty while he and Livie live at his mother's." Bennie blinked hard to hold back the tears. "He's as much as threatened he'll ask for full custody of Livie if I insist on going forward with the divorce."

"Can he do that?"

"I don't know. Maybe." Bennie hesitated and glanced at Alice's profile. "He wants my assurance there's nothing more between you and me."

Alice raked a hand through her tousled dark hair. "I can testify to that, if you need me to, but I'd have to say it's your choice, not mine."

Bennie patted Alice's hand. "You'll always be my best friend though."

Alice swung the car into a circular driveway in front of a large Colonial-style house, decorated for the season like a giant Christmas present, tied up with strings of blinking red and green lights and a huge holly wreath with a red velvet bow on the imposing front door.

"Alice, these people really take their celebrating seriously."

Parking attendants rushed to open the car doors and help the two women out.

"Be careful with it." Alice dropped the car keys into the young attendant's hand. "It's new."

The attendant grinned and saluted. "Yes, ma'am. A brand-new 1951 Packard 250 convertible. I've only seen these in pictures. She's safe with me."

Bennie and Alice walked to the front door, and Bennie shivered a little, both from the cold and with a slight feeling of dread. She expected to know many of the guests from what she was beginning to think of as her former life. She sometimes enjoyed these parties, but she suspected the business with Will would make her an object of curiosity. She pulled the collar of her coat closer around her neck.

Before Alice could ring the doorbell, the door swung open and a tall man in a bright red dinner jacket, green bow tie, and plaid cummerbund, balancing a half-full martini glass, caught Alice up in a bear hug.

"Get in here, Allie, and get something to drink. We're way ahead of you. And this beautiful blond lady is Bennie Grant, am I right?"

Alice put her arm around Bennie's waist. "I can tell you're way ahead of us, Ron. Yes, this is my friend Bennie Grant. Bennie, this is our host, Ronald Moncrieff."

Bennie stuck her hand out to shake his and ward off any bear hugs her host might have in mind for her. "How do you do, Ronald? Merry Christmas."

"I'm doing fine. Call me Ron. Come in and say hello to everyone. Here, let me take your coats."

Alice and Bennie stood in the archway on the edge of a large living room packed with women in cocktail dresses and men in black tie. Occasional high-pitched laughter floated over the noise of the crowd. A blue haze of cigarette smoke rose toward the ceiling. A mammoth Christmas tree stood by the brick fireplace with mounds of wrapped presents around its base. Bennie's eyes were drawn to the top of the tree where a delicately-poised angel seemed to survey the crowd. "You're better off up there."

Alice chuckled. "Relax." She steered Bennie into the room toward a thin woman dressed in red and green, matching Ron's outfit. She was darting among the guests, offering drinks and making introductions.

Alice introduced her friend once they caught up to the woman. "Bennie Grant, Ruth Moncrieff."

"Oh, Bennie, so glad you could come. Alice mentioned you could use some Christmas cheer. Of course, we've heard about the separation and all, and we couldn't be more sympathetic, a shame with your little girl and all. Not being ones for gossip, of course, we haven't heard all the details." Ruth took a breath and paused, looking at Bennie with an expectant smile.

Here was the curiosity Bennie anticipated. She shot Alice a glance. "Thanks so much for your hospitality. What a lovely tree."

"Oh, yes. These decorations have been in Ron's family for generations. We can't wait to pull them out every year and share them with, well, two hundred of our closest friends." Ruth looked around the noisy crowd.

Alice pointed to the bar. "Let's get a drink, Bennie."

Drink in hand, Bennie stood with two couples whom she knew from Town Players of New Canaan, the community theater group she belonged to. She watched Alice moving easily through the crowd and envied her friend's ability to enjoy a social situation. She wondered how soon she could give Alice the let's leave sign. In the meantime, she determined to make the best of the situation and joined in the polite small talk, falling back into the social dance that characterized her nine-year marriage to Will.

After a while, she excused herself from the group and slipped out the French doors leading to a patio. When the doors closed behind her, there was blessed silence, with only the muffled sounds of the party inside. Canvas covered a wrought-iron table and chairs, shrouded against the winter weather. Faint light from the house threw shadows in the garden beyond the patio. Bushes were draped with burlap bags tied with rope around their bases. The wind had loosened one of the ties and was billowing up the bush's skirt. Bennie thought of the rose bushes in the garden behind the house where she and Will and Livie once lived. Did anyone think to cover them before the weather changed?

She shivered in the cold air, took a cigarette from her purse, and lit it with a gold lighter. Bennie turned the lighter over in her hand and ran her thumb across her name engraved in fancy script. It was a gift from Will the day after they met at a debutante ball. Will told Bennie he tracked the engraver down at his home on a Sunday and convinced him to do the work. From the first dance at the ball, Will pursued her over the next weeks with the same dogged determination.

He was stationed in Washington at the War Department and began coming to New York every weekend to see Bennie. She was only nineteen, younger than Will by eight years. She was used to boys her own age being attracted by her looks, but Will was different, more settled and mature. He proposed after only three months. He had inside information that the war in Europe would soon be over, and he wanted to get a head start on their life together. He described the house they would buy in Connecticut, near his parents, the beautiful children they would have, and his position with his father's commercial real estate firm.

What he hadn't counted on was that even though Bennie was young, she already knew her own mind. Once they were married it became clear her personality was not enough of a blank slate to suit him and his mother. But then Livie came along, and he was on top of the world. He adored their daughter and turned his attention to acquiring things for her.

Someone opened the French doors and the chatter of the party spilled out onto the patio. Bennie turned to see a tall, attractive man with dark hair and a mustache smiling at her. He came to her and kissed her on the cheek.

"Bennie, I saw you come outside, and I was beginning to think you'd frozen to death. Am I interrupting?"

"No, Arthur. It's good to see you. I hadn't heard you were back from Europe. Let's go inside. It is freezing out here."

They rejoined the circle of people Bennie knew, and one of the women said, "Why, Bennie and Arthur McCall. How do you know each other?" The woman leaned forward, looking back and forth from Bennie to Arthur.

"Bennie and my sister were roommates at boarding school." Arthur took Bennie's hand and drew her away from the group. "You look as amazing as always, Bennie. You were the prettiest girl in Meg's class but never seemed to be aware of it."

"Thanks, Arthur, but I can hardly take credit for my looks. We inherit our features from our parents, right?" His hand was too warm and his grip on hers made her feel trapped. "Would you mind terribly getting me another drink?"

While he headed for the bar, Bennie scanned the room to find Alice. She saw her near the fireplace, perched on the arm of a sofa, talking to a pretty young woman smiling up at her, hanging on her every word. Alice looked across the room at Bennie and winked. Bennie was surprised to feel a small prick of emotion, jealousy or possessiveness. She frowned and mouthed, "Let's go."

Arthur came back with a Manhattan in each hand.

They sipped their drinks in awkward silence. Bennie struggled to find a neutral topic. "How's Meg?"

"She's fine. Living in DC, working for Senator Margaret Chase Smith."

"You must be very proud of her. Rightfully so."

"I am."

"Meg's invited me several times down to Washington for a visit, but I haven't managed it. I think she's given up on me."

"I doubt she'd do that."

"What about you, Arthur? Catch me up." Bennie looked across the room for Alice, but she and the young woman had disappeared.

Arthur sipped his drink. "I'm just back from Zurich. Still with the bank. What about you? You were going to be a famous Broadway director."

"I can't believe you remember that."

"I remember everything about you. Are you doing anything in the theater now?"

"I'm teaching drama at Mary Bradford's, and I've joined the community theater. We put on two productions a year, and I do everything from directing to box office to painting scenery. I sometimes even act when there's no one else for a part."

"You're at Mary Bradford's? Did you ever imagine you'd be back at your alma mater?"

"No, never."

"I hope you'll let me see you sometime. If not for dinner, then maybe a drink?" Arthur put his hand on Bennie's arm.

"Oh, Arthur. On top of being busy, I'm afraid I wouldn't be good company right now."

"I heard about the problems with your marriage. I'm a great listener, and I can be good company while you sort things out. May I call you?"

"Of course, but I won't promise."

Alice walked up, smiling at Bennie.

"Alice, this is Arthur McCall, Meg's brother. You remember Meg."

"Yes, I do. Your roommate when you were in school at Mary Bradford's. How are you, Arthur? Bennie, I'm afraid we must leave. I'm her ride, Arthur, and the bus is leaving."

They said their goodbyes, wrapped their coats around them, and stepped into the cold winter air. As they waited for the Packard to be brought around, Bennie put her arm through Alice's. "You're my hero coming to save me like that. Especially tearing yourself away from the pretty young woman you were talking to. She obviously found you fascinating. Who is she?"

"Her name is Sarah, and she's married to an assistant professor at Bridgeport. They're brand new in town."

"Alice, you're incorrigible."

"What? She's a golfer. We're going to play golf."

"In the dead of winter?"

"Well, we'll undoubtedly play golf sometime."

Chapter Two

Tuesday night, Bennie sat alone in the darkened theater at Mary Bradford School for Girls, slumped low in the seat with her feet on the back of the row in front of her. If Mother Berry, the school's headmistress, were to see her now, she'd frown on the unladylike pose.

"Not a good role model for the girls." Bennie could almost hear her saying it.

Bennie wouldn't have been able to sit up straight if Mary Bradford herself stepped out of 1845 and walked into the theater. She was bone-tired. Two days of dress rehearsals for the annual school Revel were behind her. The run-throughs had been chaos, full of missed cues and costume problems. Since working out glitches was the purpose of a dress rehearsal, Bennie hoped she and the girls had smoothed over all the mistakes and that everyone's nerves would settle once the curtain rose on the performance.

The stage in front of her was lit only by orange exit signs, but Bennie could make out the details of the set since she had lived with it day and night for weeks. At the back of the stage raised on a platform were a long banquet table and ornate chairs, the middle one larger than the rest. Potted shrubs trimmed in shapes of balls, corkscrews, and pyramids lined the sides of the set, and scarlet and gold satin drapes hid the stage lights and softened the edges of the stage.

Directing the Revel was a big responsibility, and it was important that Bennie get it right. The production was a highlight of every school year. Since the founding of the school except for a few years during the Civil War, students wrote the dialogue, costumed the actors, built the sets, and performed an original stage production. The stories were fantastical mixes of fairy tales, Shakespeare, and whatever movie was popular during the year. This year's extravaganza would have duels, dragons, witches, belly dancers, and diabolical plots. There were over a hundred girls in the cast, a third of the school, and another thirty in the orchestra.

The double doors at the back of the theater banged open. Bennie turned to see a figure silhouetted against the lights of the lobby.

"Mrs. Grant, is that you? It's black as pitch in here." It was Miss Dodie, the Latin teacher.

"Right here, Miss Dodie." Bennie sat up straighter as Miss Dodie hurried down the aisle, feeling her way in the dark, and dropped into the seat next to her.

"Thank goodness I found you. Mother Berry is looking for you. When you weren't at dinner, I figured you'd be here." Miss Dodie looked around the auditorium and pulled a pack of cigarettes from her cleavage. "Want one? I know this is strictly forbidden, but I'm so nervous. Are you? I can't wait to get this damned, sorry thing over with. Again, let me thank you for the hundredth time for taking the Revel off my shoulders in the middle of things."

"Thank you for agreeing to stay on as assistant director. I couldn't have done it without your help."

Miss Dodie took a deep drag from her cigarette and blew out the smoke, fanning the air and looking around again. "Don't get me wrong. I'm happy to be helping you with it, but let's face it, the Revel is not my cup of tea. Mother Berry assigned the thing to me before you came to teach drama because almost no one takes my Latin classes anymore. Only three girls have signed up for next term. I'm hanging on to this teaching position by a thread. Sometimes I think I should face the inevitable and get a job as a salesgirl somewhere. Maybe Bloomingdale's."

"What does Mother Berry want to see me about?" Bennie sat up straight, smoothed her skirt, and straightened the seams of her hose.

"She didn't give me any details. Please let me know after you talk to her. I wonder if it's about the belly dance. If we have to change that at the last minute, I don't know what we'll do." Miss Dodie dropped her head in her hands.

Bennie patted Miss Dodie's arm. "Don't worry. If it's the belly dance, we'll cover up the girls' midriffs. It's going to go well. We'll just have to manage whatever Mother Berry's concerned about." She stepped around Miss Dodie and headed up the aisle. "I'll find out what's up with Mother Berry and let you know if you need to get fitted for your Bloomingdale's smock."

"Don't joke about this, Mrs. Grant. It's serious," Miss Dodie called after her.

Bennie pushed through the doors, crossed the lobby, and took a deep breath before stepping into the cold wind blowing across campus.

She climbed the wide stone steps of Old Main, the school's original building. Generations of girls' hurrying feet had worn deep grooves into the stone steps. When Bennie attended school at Mary Bradford's, classes were still held in the old building, but it had been restored to house administrative offices and the board meeting room. Mother Berry's apartment was on the top floor.

Bennie took the stairs, avoiding the unreliable, creaky old elevator. At the door of the headmistress' apartment, Bennie hesitated, marshalling her arguments for leaving the belly dance in as planned. As she raised her hand to knock, the door jerked open, startling both Bennie and Mother Berry.

"Mrs. Grant, what are you doing out here? I was about to go and see if Miss Dodie had found you. Come in. This is urgent." Mother Berry pulled Bennie into the small parlor and guided her to an overstuffed chair.

Entering the apartment was like stepping into a time warp. Bennie suspected nothing had been updated since 1925 when Mother Berry came to Mary Bradford's as a young widow and took the school on as her life's preoccupation. She didn't spend money on herself, and to the consternation of the faculty, she was unwilling to pay them what they considered they were worth. Mother Berry often preached that the opportunity of teaching at Mary Bradford should be compensation enough. Bennie never joined the other teachers in grousing about their pay. She was grateful to Mother Berry for taking her on in the middle of the term when Will ordered her out of their house.

"Mrs. Grant, the Board of Trustees are coming to the Revel. We invite them every year, but it's perfunctory, and they've never shown up. I suspect our new board member is behind it. She says she wants to be much more involved, which is fine with me if she means being generous with her husband's considerable fortune, and of course, her own too. She's a successful interior designer in New York, you know."

Bennie looked around the parlor and smiled to herself. *What would a successful designer think of Mother Berry's apartment?*

"And her husband is a successful Broadway producer. You'll have that in common, given your interest in the stage. Anyway, she's the first woman board member, and the first alumna, of course. You and I both know the school attracts simply the best and brightest girls from everywhere. Mary Bradford's is the best, the best, the best, and some of our girls need financial help. Mrs. Clayborn can afford scholarships for hundreds of girls who otherwise would have no means for coming here. Plus," Mother Berry leaned toward Bennie, "we might get her interested in the improvements in the drama program that I know you'd love to put in place." Mother Berry took off her glasses and tapped her lips with her finger. "Now, let me think."

Bennie could almost hear the flipping of index cards inside Mother Berry's head where she stored information on potential donors.

"She graduated from Mary Bradford's several years before you were a student here. She would have been…" Mother Berry's eyes lit up as she discovered the correct mental index card. "Class of '29. And you were class of '40."

"Exactly right, Mother Berry. You're amazing. How can I help?"

"We'll have a reception for the board after the performance so they can meet you and Miss Dodie and the leading characters. I need the performance to go well."

"I understand how important this is, Mother Berry, and we won't let you down. The girls are ready. Miss Dodie and I guarantee a success."

"I'm counting on you to make this year's Revel the best, the best, the best." Mother Berry rose and walked Bennie to the door.

Bennie hurried down the stairs of Old Main. She began planning how she and Helen, the student in charge of costumes, could cover the belly dancers' midriffs in time for the performance.

Chapter Three

Wednesday morning Bennie pulled the belt of her trench coat tight and pressed her back against the brick wall of the New Canaan train station, seeking shelter from the chilling wind that blew down the tracks. This early, only a few commuters were boarding the train to Manhattan. Will had snorted on the phone when she insisted on taking the train in for the meeting with his lawyer rather than ride into the city with him. Even though taking the train would keep her away from her classes longer, Bennie couldn't stand the thought of the hour-long ride alone with Will.

She arrived at Grand Central Station and took the subway to lower Manhattan where the lawyer's office was located on the top floor of a cement and glass high-rise office building. The receptionist showed Bennie to a conference room where Will and his attorney, Mr. Bell, were waiting. The two men rose to their feet as Bennie came through the door. The room smelled of the antique law books lining the room on mahogany shelves and the plush leather chairs placed around a comically massive conference table. Bennie thought the room was designed to communicate substance to the client and to intimidate the adversary. Mr. Bell indicated a chair to his left.

Mr. Bell facilitated a civil discussion about how assets would be divided, should they decide to go ahead with the divorce. Bennie had expected this discussion to go smoothly. Will was a fair man, and she was confident she could count on his generous, even lavish, support of their daughter. Bennie didn't expect anything for herself. She inherited her grandmother's estate, and she cared little for the lifestyle she gave up when she moved to Mary Bradford School to teach.

Will seemed aloof and almost bored as the lawyer went through a detailed plan for distribution of their joint assets. Then the attorney changed the course of the discussion. "Now, there's the question of custody of your daughter."

When Will's eyes narrowed, a chill ran down Bennie's back. The tone of the discussion was about change as Will sat straighter in his chair. "There are some questions I need answers to before coming to any agreement about that."

Bennie clasped her hands in her lap. "What questions? What do you need to know?"

"Where you will live, for example. And with whom?"

Bennie glanced at the attorney, and because of the look on his face she suspected Will had told him of her affair with Alice. "You know I'll provide a safe and stable place for Livie. What's this about?" Bennie wanted to force Will to put things on the table.

Will's face flushed darker pink. "You know very well what it's about. I want some assurances."

The lawyer put a hand on Will's arm. "Let's stop for today and take this up at our next meeting. That will give you more time to think about what's best for the child."

***

Will and Bennie rode the elevator down in uncomfortable silence. Outside it had begun to snow, and the street and sidewalk were dusted with a thin layer of powder. A Salvation Army volunteer smiled at Bennie and nodded, his bell making a polite but insistent demand on her holiday spirit of charity. Bennie dropped a bill in the kettle. She expected Will would go on without her, but he stopped to fish several bills out of his wallet for the kettle, and then he turned to Bennie.

"Let's go someplace for a drink." Before she could reply, he took her arm.

"I can't. I have to get back to school. One of the other teachers is covering my classes."

He looked surprised and then annoyed. He hailed a cab. "We need to make some decisions. You need to decide what you want." He held the taxi door for her. "You're going to the train station, right? I'll ride with you."

Bennie hesitated. "No need. I'll take the subway."

Will shook his head, waved the cab away, and set off down the street on foot.

Chapter Four

Bennie peeked through the heavy velvet stage curtain at the stream of students, parents, and townspeople filling the aisles and seats of the auditorium. Mother Berry had reserved the front two rows for board members and their wives. The board members were dressed in almost identical three-piece business suits and their wives in hats and gloves.

The thirty-piece orchestra was arranged in a semi-circle in front of the stage. Mr. Crump, the school's music teacher, paced back and forth between the violins and cellos, stopping often to shuffle the score pages on his podium.

When everyone appeared settled, Miss Dodie gave Bennie the sign that all the actors were in their spots and ready for the curtain. Bennie took a last peek at the audience before pulling the curtain. A tall woman in a mink pushed through the auditorium doors and hesitated beside an empty seat in the last row. Mother Berry half rose and motioned to a seat in the front row, and the woman rushed forward. Bennie thought this must be the famous new board member, Mrs. Clayborn. Mr. Crump struck up the overture, Bennie pulled the curtain rope, and the Revel began.

For the next two hours the audience watched a story of court intrigue set in Elizabethan times. Would-be suitors fought duels in futile attempts to win the Queen's hand. Between sword fights, dancers from faraway lands in skimpy costumes gyrated to the sounds of flutes and drums and witches cast spells around a simulated bonfire. Wild applause from the audience interrupted the performance regularly.

After the actors took three curtain calls, Miss Dodie collapsed in Bennie's arms. "Thank God it's over and none of the mistakes made a bit of difference. I swear we could throw up any drivel and no one would care. Now if we can get through this board reception, I can relax for the first time since September."

Bennie began gathering up props. "I thoroughly enjoyed it. I even shed a few tears. I'm so proud of the girls."

"Maybe I am better suited for Bloomingdale's after all."

Bennie and Miss Dodie walked across campus to Old Main to join the board reception. Bennie paused at the top of the stairs. "You go ahead. I'm going to catch my breath and enjoy the view for a minute."

She sat on the top step and looked across the school's wooded thirty-acre campus on the highest point in New Canaan, with a vista over the Connecticut River toward Long Island Sound. Bennie drew a deep breath and pushed herself up from the step, ready as she would ever be for her command performance. The massive doors leading into the boardroom stood open for the reception. Four members of the orchestra, recruited as a string quartet, were attempting Vivaldi but sounded worn out from their performance in the Revel. Conversation buzzed among the faculty and student cast members.

Bennie paused at the doorway and surveyed the scene. A roaring fire reflected off the highly polished, old hardwood floor. Several middle-aged men clustered in the center of the room, laughing at someone's joke. Bennie recognized a few of them from the country club and various business functions she had attended with Will. Apart from the men, in a group of their own, expensively dressed wives of the board members chatted. In the middle of the circle of board members, stood one lone woman. She was the center of attention and appeared to be the one whose joke caused them to laugh. She wore a Chanel suit, and she held back the jacket with a hand on her waist. The woman seemed comfortable in the men's presence, not the least bit deferential or flirtatious. Bennie thought she was magnificent.

One of the men chuckled heartily. "Well, I for one am glad to have a woman's point of view on the board. We men know how to make the money, but you ladies know how to spend it." He laughed through the awkward silence that followed.

The woman smiled at him. "I suppose the key for the school is to keep those two things in a healthy balance, and I'll try to keep up my end of that equation."

The other men smiled and chuckled.

Mother Berry rushed over to Bennie. "Here you are, dear. I was wondering where you had gotten off to. Come and speak to the board members." Mother Berry took Bennie's elbow and instead of introducing her to the circle of men, she steered her directly toward the woman. "Mrs. Clayborn, this is Mrs. Grant, the director of our Revel and the drama teacher I was telling you about. She's also the absolute backbone of our wonderful community theater in New Canaan. In her short time here at Mary Bradford's, she has made our drama department the best, the best, the best, and she can do so much more with a few additional resources." Mother Berry spied a prosperous-looking couple just coming in the door. "Bennie, tell Mrs. Clayburn your ideas." She bustled away toward the couple.

Bennie was embarrassed by Mother Berry's brazen fundraising pitch. She studied Mrs. Clayborn's face for a negative reaction, but the woman turned to Bennie with a look of genuine interest and curiosity and extended her hand. "I'm Laura."

Up close, her features were too strong to be called classically beautiful. Her nose and mouth were slightly large, and her dark eyes a little too close together, yet the whole effect was arresting. Touching the woman's hand caused a rush of emotion that made Bennie's head buzz and heart skip a beat.

She managed a reply. "I'm Bennie Grant." Bennie realized she was still holding Laura's hand. She dropped it and felt her cheeks flush. "I'm pleased to meet you. Mother Berry told me the board added a new member, a woman. I hope you enjoyed the Revel and thank you for coming." Bennie felt her blush deepen as she rattled on.

"I enjoyed the Revel very much, Bennie. This is my first school event as a board member, and I'm impressed." Her voice was a soft alto, with a hint of a Southern accent. "I'm especially impressed with how well the production was put together, and that's thanks to you, I suppose."

"Miss Dodie and myself. And of course, the girls played all the important roles, on the stage and with the production. Mother Berry mentioned you went to school here. You must have worked on the Revel, too, in your day."

Laura grimaced. "'In my day' makes me sound ancient."

Bennie swallowed hard, afraid she had insulted her, but to her relief, Laura smiled. "We couldn't avoid working on the Revel. I built sets, and senior year I was in charge of set design for a perfectly awful musical version of *Romeo and Juliet*."

Bennie saw Mother Berry glance across the room and nod, reminding her of the headmistress's motive for introducing Laura to her— to fuel the new board member's interest in financial support for the school.

"As Mother Berry said, I've taken over teaching drama." Her voice sounded awkward and overeager. "I mean to say, I would appreciate any advice you or your husband might have about how to make the program better."

Laura smiled and nodded. "We do want to do our part to make sure Mary Bradford's stays the best, the best, the best, to use Mother Berry's mantra. Let's meet sometime to talk about your ideas in more detail. I'm in the city during the week but often in New Canaan on the weekends. Shall we have dinner sometime?"

Before Bennie could respond, Mother Berry interrupted to whisk Laura away to meet the couple who just arrived. Undoubtedly more potential donors. Bennie wandered to the refreshment table and ladled some day-glow-green punch from a large, crystal bowl into a tiny cup, found the liquid too sweet to drink, and opted for coffee instead.

She drifted over to encourage the string quartet and found herself surrounded by the girls who played leading parts in the Revel. They were high on adrenalin from the performance, chattering and vying for her attention, half-seriously lobbying for canceling class on Monday.

Bennie watched Laura move around the room, introducing herself to teachers and students. Laura focused on each person she met, almost as though being interested was her job, which Bennie supposed, as a board member, it was. When she had worked her way around the crowd, Laura gathered her coat and gloves and approached Mother Berry. She nodded several times in response to Mother Berry's effusive thanks. Then she looked across the room, directly into Bennie's eyes, smiled, waved goodbye, and was gone.

Chapter Five

Bennie found herself struggling to drag herself out of bed on Monday morning. Half asleep, she made her bed by rote and stumbled into her tiny bathroom for a shower. The private bath was the one civilized feature of her dorm mother room. She lacked a private telephone and had to depend on the stuffy booth in the hallway all the girls on her floor shared. It was tolerable since Bennie used the phone only to talk to Livie, and sometimes Alice. She had no other social life.

There were three days left until school closed for the holidays. The dorm was noisy around the clock as the girls anticipated their trips home. Bennie had hardly slept since the Revel, but her insomnia was not just the girls' fault. Laura Clayborn was another reason she tossed all night.

Bennie played the scene at the board reception over in her head—Laura's way with people, her gestures, and especially the smile and wave as she left. The look made Bennie feel the woman could see right through Bennie to her yearning to know her better.

She rushed to be on time for Shakespeare class, barely beating the bell into her classroom. In the spring, the massive double-hung windows of her room in the old building were thrown open to pleasant breezes and smells from the countryside. Today, the windows were shut against the cold, and the room smelled of damp wool and chalk dust.

She had the students read aloud from *King Lear*. She leaned against her desk, trying to stay alert, listening with a fixed smile. She daydreamed about how she would create a modern-day staging of Lear and whom she would cast in the parts. The metallic knocking of the radiator under one of the windows startled her out of her reverie. Mercifully, the end of period bell sounded. The girls grabbed their books and stampeded toward the door, almost trampling Mother Berry's secretary in the doorway.

The woman hugged herself and closed her eyes as the girls thundered past. Once it was safe, she walked to Bennie's desk. "Mrs. Grant, Mother Berry asked me to deliver this phone message." The secretary held her hands behind her back as though she were going to make Bennie guess which hand. "I would normally put the message in your cubby-hole, but when I told Mother Berry that a board member had called specifically for you, she felt I should deliver it to your classroom. So here it is." She slapped the paper on Bennie's desk and left.

Bennie fumbled as she unfolded the piece of paper. The typed note said, *Mrs. Clayborn called. Asked you to call her back at your convenience.* At the bottom was a Manhattan phone number. Bennie refolded the message and put it in her sweater pocket.

The day dragged on. Bennie struggled to concentrate on her classes. She checked the big clock above the blackboard often. When her last period was over, she hurried back to the residence hall and waited impatiently for the girls to go to dinner. Once things were quiet, Bennie sat in the telephone alcove with the message smoothed on her knee. She took a deep breath and dialed the number. After the fifth ring without an answer, she was about to hang up.

"Hello? Hello?" Laura's voice sounded strained and out of breath.

"Mrs. Clayborn, this is Bennie Grant from Mary Bradford's. I can call back if this is a bad time."

There was a pause on the other end of the line. Bennie had the sinking feeling Laura had forgotten about the call, or the secretary in Mother Berry's office had gotten the message wrong. Bennie's mind flashed back to Laura standing with her coat over her arm, preparing to leave the board reception. The look that seemed so personal to Bennie was just Laura being polite.

"Of course, Bennie. Thank you for calling back. Sorry I took so long to answer the phone. I thought Sophia would get it, but she must have gone out."

Bennie had no idea who Sophia was or what to say next. "Yes."

"I called to invite you for dinner to discuss the drama program. I'll be in New Canaan the weekend after Christmas. Maybe you can come to my weekend place that Saturday. You'll still be on holiday, I think. I can pick you up at the school. If you're free, that is."

Bennie squeezed her eyes shut and gripped the telephone receiver. "I am free." She struggled to keep her voice level. "I'd love to come to dinner."

They arranged to meet in front of the residence hall a week from Saturday.

Chapter Six

Thursday, classes were over for the holidays. All but a few senior girls had left for their homes or for trips with their parents. Bennie settled down on her narrow bed to wrap Livie's Christmas present. She held the life-sized doll at arm's length and admired her real-hair wig and her cornflower blue eyes that closed when she was laid down. She had been especially careful picking out the doll because she suspected it might be the last one Livie would want. Next Christmas she would ask for more grown-up things.

Livie already preferred her gifts wrapped in what she called grown-up paper and real bows. Since she was a little girl, she enjoyed opening her presents as much as the presents themselves. She always carefully untied the ribbons and smoothed them out with her tiny hands before deliberately loosening the paper, careful not to tear it. Only after she watched Bennie neatly fold the paper was she ready to look what was inside.

Bennie finished wrapping the doll and turned to the small, robin's-egg blue box that held a gold lapel pin she had bought for Alice. The pin was a tiny hummingbird with a ruby eye, her wings spread in flight. Alice had majored in ornithology in college. When Bennie teased her about choosing such an esoteric area to study, Alice said, "Oh, I'm not interested in the science of it. I like the birds' personalities." Bennie wrote a note thanking Alice for her friendship, especially during the difficulty with Will, and wrapped the note and the box in brown paper for mailing.

Bennie planned to take Livie's doll to Will's mother's that afternoon to put under the Christmas tree. She was excited about a visit with her child but was apprehensive about seeing Will's mother. Bennie hadn't been alone with Olivia since the separation.

She asked the taxi driver to let her off at the iron gates guarding the long drive up to the main house. She hoped the walk would calm her nerves and prepare her for what might be a confrontational scene with Olivia. As she walked up the winding gravel road, she remembered the first time Will brought her to meet his mother ten years before. It was in the spring, and the woods were full of dogwood and hydrangeas in bloom. Bennie was madly in love, and she and Will were already talking of marriage.

She stopped to catch her breath and shifted the weight of Livie's gift, careful not to flatten the bow. As she rounded the last bend in the drive, the woods gave way to the front gardens. She paused again to admire the house's façade. The stately mansion was made of brick and stucco with half-timbers and a steeply pitched roof with ten chimneys, each topped with a decorative chimney pot. In front, evergreens dominated the English garden in the winter, presided over by a massive pine tree, decorated with lights for the holidays. This view of the Grant mansion always made her think that somehow grand houses in New England were more substantial than in other places, as though they'd had more time to become rooted to the earth.

She climbed the broad cement front steps, and steady old Haskins, the Grants' butler, opened the front door. "It's good to see you, Mrs. Grant."

"It's good to see you, too, Haskins. It's been a while."

Haskins led the way into the parlor where a twelve-foot Christmas tree filled a corner of the room. Bennie added Livie's doll to the mountain of gifts under the tree.

Haskins stood back with his hands folded, smiling at Bennie. "May I help you with anything else, Mrs. Grant?"

"Do you remember the first time I came here, Haskins?"

"I certainly do, Mrs. Grant."

Bennie thought of the subtle and unexpected scrutiny by Will's mother during dinner that first evening and how their conversation had become like a well-played tennis match, Olivia lobbing polite questions about her family, upbringing, schooling, likes and dislikes, and Bennie receiving and responding. To anyone listening, it would have seemed that Olivia Grant was a gracious and interested hostess, but Bennie knew she had been thoroughly auditioned for the important role of Will's wife.

Haskins brought Bennie back to the present. "Mrs. Grant and Miss Livie are in the library."

"Thank you, Haskins. I can find my way."

Her heels clicking on the polished quarter-sawn oak floor announced her coming, and before she reached the library door, Livie came bounding out and into her arms. The sight of her beautiful blond child made Bennie's heart leap with love.

"Mama, you're here. Grandmother and I are reading *The Night Before Christmas*, though it's technically not. It's really Christmas Eve eve."

Bennie knelt to look into the child's eyes. "Livie, slow down and let me give you a proper hug and kiss. I've missed you these last few days."

"I know. Me too. Did you see the tree on the front lawn? The lights are up, but we won't turn them on until it's actually Christmas, which happens at 12:01 tomorrow night. Grandmother is going to let me stay up and flip the switch if Daddy says it's okay, and we think he will."

"And, of course, if your mother approves." Olivia stood in the library doorway, watching mother and daughter.

Bennie rose but held on to Livie's hand. She took in Olivia's well-maintained, old-money looks and thought, as she had many times, that they could be taken for mother and daughter, or maybe even older and younger sisters. She and Olivia had the same pale blonde hair, hazel eyes, and slim figure.

"Hello, Olivia."

"We're having some tea and reading to each other." Olivia motioned into the room. "Please, join us."

Livie led her mother into the library and to the sofa. The room was comfortable with bookshelves lining the walls, floor to ceiling, and a large rock fireplace on the east wall. A fire burning brightly in the fireplace warmed the whole room. Bennie thought the library looked like a stage set, the perfect picture, just as Olivia herself.

Olivia poured tea for Bennie and took her own cup to sit behind the ornately-carved mahogany desk in front of a large window looking out over the back gardens sloping down to the woods.

Livie squirmed onto the sofa next to her mother. "We'll sit here, and I'll read to you." She opened the book. "'Twas the night before Christmas." She stopped reading and positioned the book so Bennie could see the page. "'Twas means it was. That's the funny way they used to say it." Livie read the poem through with only a few prompts from Bennie, the child's brows knit together with her focus on getting the words just right.

Bennie smoothed away the concentration lines between Livie's brows with her thumbs. "You read that so well, darling."

"I mostly have it memorized."

Olivia sipped her tea. "Livie, will you take your book up to your room now, so your mother and I can have a talk?"

Bennie was disappointed to give up time with her daughter, but she knew this talk would come sooner or later. Bennie took a deep breath and hugged Livie, then hugged her closer. "I'll call you tomorrow and see you day after tomorrow, baby."

After Livie had gone, Olivia rose from the desk and turned toward the window to gaze at the woods, her back to Bennie. "This isn't an easy discussion to have."

"No."

"Will has confided in me about your...your incident with Alice Gifford. I won't ask you the details. I don't want to know them."

"I'm glad to hear you don't want to spend time talking about Alice and me because, Olivia, that's not why Will and I have separated. When Will was confiding in you, I would have thought he would tell you we've both been unhappy almost from the day we married."

Olivia turned toward Bennie. "You are responsible for that."

"I'll certainly take half the responsibility. My defense is that I was very young and in love for the first time. I didn't anticipate that Will, or marriage, or his family, would require me to be someone I'm not. I naively believed he would be who he was, or who I thought he was anyway, and I would be who I was, and that we'd live happily ever after with three or four beautiful children." Bennie began to cry. "By the time I began to understand that his quest to change me into his picture of a wife would never stop, that we would never grow out of it or endure through it, we had Livie, and I tried to find a way to live in it, but I can't."

Olivia pulled a tissue from her sweater sleeve and walked around the desk to hand it to Bennie, then returned to her chair. "You must find a way to live with your responsibilities. Do you think you're the only woman who's ever had to put her marriage and family before her own yearnings and temptations?" Olivia's mouth was a thin, tight line, the same look Will had when he was angry. "Haven't we, hasn't Will, given you every advantage for a fulfilling life? You've had your work with the community theater and whatever else you fancied, as well as your child. I don't understand how you can throw your life away for some adolescent crush."

"Olivia, I despair of convincing you that Alice had nothing to do with this. Where is this conversation going?"

Olivia rose and leaned forward, her hands clutched in tight fists. "All right, let's put our cards on the table. I know my son is willing to overlook some very destructive things you've done. You have the power, and the responsibility, to repair your marriage, for him, Livie, and all of us. Give up this ridiculous nonsense of teaching or someday directing plays, or whatever you're thinking. You've chosen to be a wife and mother. And, most importantly, you must give us assurances that Alice is a thing of the past."

Bennie heard the word again that Will had used in the lawyer's office, assurances.

"If you don't, we'll petition for full custody. You'll be giving Livie up."

Olivia's words hung in the silence between them. The threat Will had hinted at was out in the open. In a way, Bennie envied Olivia's certainty of right and wrong. How does a person become so sure?

"Olivia, don't mistake my emotions for weakness. When it comes to my child, you can't even begin to imagine my strength. I'll never hurt Livie, and I won't be threatened. I'll never abandon her, and I'll never use her, and I'm certain Will won't either. We'll do the best we can for her."

Olivia turned her back again. "You may not agree on what the best is. Think about what I've said, Bennie. I won't stand idly by and let my son and my grandchild be hurt."

Chapter Seven

The next day was Christmas Eve. Bennie's residence hall floor was eerily quiet. She checked on the few girls staying at school over the holidays. They were on their beds or sitting at their desks, reading or listening to the radio. They seemed as content as Bennie to spend the time alone in their rooms. At ten o'clock, Bennie was preparing to turn off her light for the night when the phone rang, shrill and amplified by the walls of the booth in the hallway. She tried ignoring the jangle but whoever was calling let it ring over and over, refusing to take no for an answer. She finally ran out to answer. "Yes?"

"It's me," Will said.

Bennie heard party noises in the background. She could tell from his slurred speech he had been drinking. She tried to keep the impatience out of her voice, hoping to avoid a confrontation on the phone. "What is it, Will?"

"I'm at the club, and I have a little something for you for Christmas, and I want to bring it by."

"That's not possible. It's late, and everything's closed up for the holidays."

"It won't take a minute. You can meet me downstairs. I'll run in and run out." The line went dead.

For a moment, she stood holding the dead receiver to her ear, paralyzed by a deep, helpless anger at Will's assumption he could call at this late hour and dictate she see him. "Damn him."

Bennie barely managed to pull on some slacks and a sweater and get downstairs before she heard the crunching of tires on the gravel followed by Will's knock on the front door.

"Hello, Bennie. Where can we sit?"

"It's too late for this, and it's Christmas Eve."

"Exactly. Almost Merry Christmas." He pushed through the door and turned left into the formal parlor, finding the light switch inside the door. "Here we are. This will do."

He took off his overcoat and flung it on a sofa, as familiar as though he were in his own living room. He pulled a silver flask from his jacket pocket and offered it to Bennie. "Want one?"

His eyebrows rose with the question. Bennie noticed how the left one was peaked in the middle because of an old scar from a riding accident. When they met, she thought the blemish gave him a rakish air, and after a while, she stopped even noticing it. Tonight, the scar made him look malevolent, and she was angry with herself for feeling a little afraid of him. Bennie shook her head.

"Suit yourself." Will sat heavily on the sofa beside his coat, crossed his legs, and straightened the crease of his pants. "So you're spending Christmas Eve alone."

Bennie closed the double pocket doors separating the parlor from the reception area and leaned against them. "Does it occur to you that since we're separated, it's really none of your business how I spend my time?"

"Being separated is not my choice. You demanded a divorce."

"And you threw me out of the house." Bennie hugged herself in the chilly room. "After I told you about Alice, you couldn't get me out fast enough. Were you afraid your friends at the club would find out and somehow connect you with my depravity?"

"To tell you the truth, I don't take the Alice thing very seriously. Two women together? What do two women do in bed anyway? I've often wondered." He smirked. "I'd guess Alice was the 'man.'"

Bennie balled her fists and bit her lower lip. "You're drunk and disgusting. Get on with what you came for and get out."

He settled back on the sofa. "What's old Alice up to lately anyhow?"

"I won't go through this with you."

She turned and began opening the doors. Will sprang off the sofa so quickly he caught Bennie off balance. He pushed her away from the doors and slammed them shut.

"Will, you're in my place of work." Bennie hoped appealing to his business mind might calm Will down. "I can't have you here right now."

"Relax." He put his palms up in an exaggerated gesture and looked around. "This place is as empty as a tomb." He sat again on the sofa. "So have you seen her lately?"

"Again, that's none of your concern."

"It's my concern when it involves Livie, and I won't have you exposing my daughter to who knows what odd leanings you have."

"You can't really imagine I'd do anything to hurt Livie. You know me better than that."

Will stared at Bennie for a moment, and then his face softened. Bennie recognized the emotion on his face. He saw her as he had when they got along. "I thought I knew you. I know Livie loves you and you love her. I'm willing to believe we can work out what's best for her. It's best that both of us are in her life, and in order to agree to that, I need assurances you've put all this behind you. I know how these things go. I suspect Alice has had these feelings for you her whole life. I may have been too preoccupied with work. The situation was partly my fault. I should have put a stop to your spending so much time with her. You see, I'm not a total Neanderthal."

Bennie shook her head and smiled to herself. Could Will really believe he could have prevented her affair with Alice by simply dictating it to her?

"You and Olivia keep bringing up your need for assurances. What specific assurances?"

"That things are over between you and Alice, and that you won't bring any of these influences around Livie."

"I can give you those assurances."

"Good. Then I have a proposal for you." Will sat forward eagerly, as though negotiating a business deal. "I want to put our marriage back together. Being a family is best for our child, and I'm convinced you'll come to see it's best for all of us."

Bennie heard the echo of Olivia's words from their talk the day before. She sat heavily in a chair by the empty fireplace. She felt too tired to go on.

"Hear me out." Will stood and paced. "Let's have a cooling off period, say six months. That would take us to the end of the school term, both for Livie and for you. If, after a little time, you are still bent on divorcing, I'll not contest your request, and I'll agree to share custody with you, say three months alternating between us. In the meantime, Livie will stay with me at Mother's, and you can see her there anytime you want."

"No! No, I can't stand that. I want her with me."

"Be realistic, Bennie." Will made a gesture that took in the parlor. "You don't even have a proper place for her."

"I plan to get an apartment for us."

Will went on as though she hadn't spoken. "Besides, I'm surprising her with a pony for Christmas, and she's going to be obsessed with him anyway. My proposal will give you and me time to put some distance between the past and the future."

"And if I don't agree to a six-month pause with the divorce, what then?"

"Then it's my responsibility as a father to take the cautious approach and fight you for full custody. You can't really doubt what the outcome of such a fight would be."

"So you're blackmailing me."

"Listen, it won't profit you to try and make me the bad guy in this business, Bennie. I'm willing to overlook some pretty hurtful actions on your part for the sake of our family and our child's future. The least you can do is work with me on this."

"What I don't understand, Will, is why. Why do you want to hold on with a death grip to our marriage that has been making us both unhappy for so long?"

Will took another sip from the flask and fixed Bennie with cold, hard eyes. "It's not my habit to fail."

Bennie's breath caught in her throat. She could never go back into the marriage, but she knew Will would do whatever necessary to have these next few months his way. She was done. She felt tears of anger and frustration sting her eyes, but held them in, determined not to let him see her cry. "All right, I agree to your terms, but I'm still picking her up tomorrow to spend Christmas Day with me, as we have agreed. After tomorrow, Livie will stay with you at your mother's for six months, until June 24. Then we'll go forward with the divorce, and you'll agree to equal custody."

Bennie felt as though she was negotiating a business deal in which the other side held all the advantages. She had the sinking thought the rest of their lives might feel this way.

"If you're still determined to break up our family after that time, and if I can feel confident that Livie will be well provided for, then yes." Will looked around the parlor. "Ugh, this is really a drab, old building, isn't it?" He grabbed his overcoat and headed for the parlor doors. "I'll call the lawyer and tell him you and I have made a decision."

She locked the front door of the residence hall behind Will and listened for his car to drive away. Bennie remembered his excuse for coming over had been to bring her a gift for Christmas. She turned out the lights on the Christmas tree in the reception area and started to climb the stairs to the fourth floor. She sat heavily on a step with her head in her hands. "Merry Christmas."

Chapter Eight

Christmas morning dawned windy, cold, and overcast. After breakfast alone in the empty dining room, Bennie called a taxi for the ride to the Grant mansion. Occasional spits of snow splattered the windshield as the driver wound slowly up the driveway, careful to avoid icy patches that once or twice threatened to send them careening off the road.

Haskins held an umbrella over her and helped her out of the car. "They're down at the stables, Mrs. Grant."

"In this weather?"

"Miss Livie can't bear to be away from her new pony. I was about to take some hot chocolate down to them."

"I'll take it."

When Bennie got to the stable, she found Livie decked out in riding boots, jodhpurs, and a helmet, sitting astride a brown and white pinto pony. Will held the bridle and Olivia stood by beaming.

"Mama, look at him! I can't ride this morning, but maybe this afternoon if it stops snowing. His name is Dasher, like in *The Night Before Christmas.* And Grandmother got me the boots and things."

"He's very handsome, baby." Bennie suspected the doll she brought Livie had been overshadowed.

"Can we stay 'til this afternoon to see if it stops snowing? Please?"

Will and Olivia turned to her in unison, waiting for her answer, their expressions impassive. Will had been right. Livie was obsessed with the pony. Bennie didn't have the heart to insist that Livie leave her new pony to spend the time with her at Mary Bradford's.

"If you come to the house now and show me the rest of your presents, you may stay."

Olivia smiled and took Bennie's arm as they started toward the house. "This is a very good decision, my dear."

Bennie glanced at Olivia. She knew her mother-in-law wasn't referring to her decision about Livie and the pony. She meant Bennie's agreement to the six-month cooling off period. Olivia was probably the one behind the proposal. She was glad Olivia's statement didn't need a response. She doubted she could give a civil one.

***

Christmas dinner in the residence hall dining room seemed to go on forever. Bennie would rather have skipped it since Livie wasn't there to share the meal, but Mother Berry asked her to gather the few girls who were staying at school over the holidays for what the headmistress called, "Just one big happy, Mary Bradford family Christmas dinner." The kitchen staff pushed two tables together so that the fifteen girls, Mother Berry, Miss Dodie, and Bennie could sit together.

The meal seemed to move in slow motion. After the servers had finally cleared away the last plate, and Bennie was about to make her getaway, Mother Berry insisted they go around the table and share their favorite Christmas memory. The girls squirmed in their seats and looked to Bennie as if to say, "Save us." Finally, the last girl had told her story. Bennie pushed her chair back with a loud scrape that echoed in the nearly-empty room. "Well, girls, Merry Christmas 1950."

Back in her room, Bennie changed into a nightgown and robe and settled on her bed to read Tennessee Williams' latest play, *Summer and Smoke,* but she couldn't concentrate. She found the heroine's indecision tedious beyond endurance. She went to sleep with the bedside lamp on and the book lying on her stomach.

The insistent jangling of the telephone woke her early the next morning. It was Alice.

"Hello, gorgeous. Merry Day After Christmas. I opened my birdie, and she's sitting on my lapel right now, chirping her little heart out. Thank you. I have something for you, too, but you know how bad I am about the mail."

Bennie rubbed her eyes. "What are you doing up this early?"

"Long story. How was your Christmas? How is Livie?"

"That's a long story too. Just a minute, Alice."

Bennie set the phone down and tiptoed down the hallway, listening at each door to make sure the girls were still asleep.

"I'm back. I'm sorry but you know I don't have any privacy."

"I know. I don't understand why you don't get your own phone, or why you're there at all. You know you're welcome to stay with Mother and me. This house is huge. You'd practically have your own apartment. But we've been through all this. Don't let me preach at you."

"Thank you for that. Your long story doesn't have anything to do with your young golfer friend from the cocktail party the other night, Sarah Bridgeport, wasn't it?"

"Sarah *from* Bridgeport, not Sarah Bridgeport. But you tell me your long story first."

Bennie recounted Will's late-night visit and the deal she made with him with the hope of getting his agreement on shared custody of Livie. "So for the next six months, I have to live with talking to Livie on the phone or visiting her in the company of Olivia. And no finality of divorce until after June."

"Please tell me I'm not the cause of all this."

Bennie shook her head. "We've been through all that before." Bennie felt impatient with Alice. Things were difficult enough for her without all the adults in her life needing assurances of her thoughts, feelings, and future actions. She took a deep breath. "No, Alice. You're not the cause of it. You were a symptom."

"That makes me feel a little better, but not much. You make me sound like a skin rash."

Bennie laughed out loud. She peered around the corner to be sure the girls' doors were still closed. "What are you up to this week?"

"I'm going to a house party in Southampton, but I'll be back on Friday. Let me take you to dinner on Saturday."

"I've already got a date."

"A date? Not with the mustache from the cocktail party." Alice's voice showed her disappointment.

"No, I'm teasing. It's not a date. I'm having dinner with one of the board members. Mother Berry has me shilling for money to support the drama department. The board member invited me to her house for dinner."

"Her house? That stuffy group of old men added a woman to their hallowed ranks? Who is she?"

"Laura Clayborn, the interior decorator."

"Oh, ho."

"What do you mean, 'oh, ho'? Do you know her?"

"Well, I've met her, and I certainly know of her. She probably wouldn't remember me. I'm not her type."

"That's a catty thing to say. I found her impressive. What do you mean you're not her type? Where did you meet her?"

"Another long story that I'll tell you the next time I see you. I don't mean to be catty. Maybe I'm a little jealous you're seeing her for dinner instead of me. I'm sure she's going to be a big supporter of the school.

Since your social calendar is full, I'm putting your Christmas present in the mail today. Better late than never. And I'm trying not to be jealous."

Alice was deliberately steering the conversation away from telling her where she met Laura Clayborn. Bennie was determined to pursue it when she had more privacy.

Chapter Nine

Saturday afternoon, Bennie looked at the clock on her bedside table. Only five minutes had passed since she checked it last. She still had twenty minutes until Laura was due to pick her up in front of the residence hall. She filled the morning hours by talking with Livie on the phone, doing laundry in the residence hall basement, and taking a long, relaxing bath.

She stood with her back to the open door of her room, folding her fresh laundry. She jumped at the sound of a knock and whirled around to find Laura framed by the doorway. Bennie's hand flew to her mouth. She had contemplated meeting Laura again sitting across from her in the car. She was unprepared to have Laura appear in her room.

Bennie saw the puzzled look on Laura's face as she retreated a few steps.

"Bennie? It is you, isn't it? I was early, so I thought I'd come in and see the old place again. I hope I'm not intruding."

"Of course it's me. You're not intruding."

"Good." Laura threw her coat on the bed. "I'll go have a look around while you finish."

By the time Bennie had stuffed her clean laundry in a drawer, Laura was back.

"The place looks just the same, except smaller than I remember. I suppose a girls' school communal bathroom doesn't change much though."

Laura looked around Bennie's room at the sparse furnishings. She walked to the bookshelf and ran her finger along the spines. "Do you teach all these or are plays your passion?"

"I mainly teach Shakespeare and the classics."

"But it seems you like the modern playwrights—Lillian Hellman, Arthur Miller, and Tennessee Williams. I may not be intellectual enough for you."

Bennie felt a rush of pleasure. She was flattered Laura might care what she thought of her intellect. "Is your passion interior design?"

Laura drew her coat on in one graceful motion. "Let's talk about that on the road, if we must." She helped Bennie with her jacket and left her hand on Bennie's elbow as they went down the stairs side by side. On the ground floor, Laura stopped in front of the arched entrance leading to the dining room.

"How I hated meals in this room. Is it still so regimented? We had to take turns at the head of the table, playing Mother. Always pass the food to the right and stay seated until everyone finished eating."

Bennie nodded. "It's still like that."

"I skipped meals as often as possible. I existed on the peanut butter and crackers I hid in my sock drawer even though I knew it was against the rules. Mother Berry claimed the rule was to discourage mice, but I was sure the restrictions were designed to turn us into cardboard cut-outs of traditional women."

Laura swung the front door open and held it for Bennie. The day was sunny, and the air was so still and cold Bennie could imagine cracking it like a sheet of ice. Laura's long sedan was parked in the circle drive in front of the residence hall.

Bennie hoped Laura would take up the conversation about her passions once they were in the car and headed down the hill. Instead, Laura pointed out historic homes that had been restored to their pre-Revolutionary War conditions. She knew who owned them, both in the 1700s and now, and whether the current owners had done a credible job of restoration.

Bennie studied Laura's profile. "I think architecture is your passion."

Laura glanced at her. "You might be right. I became a designer because studying architecture was too unconventional for a woman. Does that make you think less of me?" Laura spoke in an offhand tone, but Bennie sensed sincerity in the question.

"You don't seem to be someone who pays attention to convention."

Laura stared straight ahead.

Bennie was afraid her comment was too personal. She might have stepped over a line. Laura might be wishing she'd never invited her to dinner. At any moment she could swing the car around and take Laura back to the school.

Laura finally responded. "I don't always pay attention to convention."

In downtown New Canaan, the crowds of pedestrians on Main Street seemed reluctant to give up the holiday spirit. Santas with sleighs and reindeer still rose from each streetlight pole, and carols rang out from the bell tower of the First Presbyterian Church. About five minutes past the village, Laura turned into a drive blocked by a gate suspended between two large brick obelisks. She rolled down her window and pressed a code on a keypad outside the gate. An automatic opener swung the gate open.

"It's magic." Bennie clapped her hands.

"The latest thing." Laura guided the car up the drive between low rock walls. They crested the hill, and a perfectly square structure made entirely of glass came into view. The effect was so dramatic that Bennie gasped.

Laura smiled. "See? Unconventional."

Laura parked the car and led Bennie across the geometrically laid out gravel paths that created a pattern in the snow-covered front lawn. The house was built with steel beams painted charcoal grey, and floor-to-roof glass walls. Inside, the floor was brick, laid in a herringbone pattern. Everywhere were clean lines. To the right of the front door, a low walnut cabinet divided the space to create a bed area.

To the left was a stainless-steel kitchen with a view of the back of the property. The living/dining area was furnished with black leather and chrome sofas and chairs and glass-topped tables. An easel near the fireplace held a large painting of a pastoral scene. The house seemed designed to be a piece of magical minimalist art, starkly and beautifully simple.

"I had no idea this house was here. Did you design it?"

"Yes. I had some help with the engineering aspects, but it was my vision of a place in harmony with its surroundings that we pursued. We finished construction in the fall."

In the gathering twilight, Bennie could still make out the surrounding woods and a pond in the back, frozen over at this time of year. She walked to the windows. "The outdoors is your wallpaper."

"Yes, I suppose you're right." Laura looked at Bennie with a slight smile. "That's an astute observation."

They had a simple supper of tomato soup and chicken salad with warm, crusty bread. After the meal, Laura poured brandies for each of them and invited Bennie to join her on the sofa.

"Now, tell me more about your passion for the theater."

"You mean the drama program at Mary Bradford's?"

"No, we can talk about that any time. I do intend to make a gift, now I'm on the board, but Mother Berry and I can work out those details. Tell me more about you. How did you become interested in acting?"

"I'm not interested in acting. I do a little of it with the community theater when I must, but my interest is in directing."

"I apologize. I made an assumption. I thought with your beauty…" Laura gently tucked a strand of Bennie's hair behind her ear. "I thought you'd be on the stage rather than in the wings. Do you forgive me?"

Bennie felt a blush creeping up her neck. "Of course."

"Tell me how you became interested in directing."

"I remember my grandmother reading to me. I pictured the characters acting out their parts, and, when I could read on my own, the stories turned into plays. I imagined the creative process that would give an audience, and the cast and crew, a memorable experience." She stopped, out of breath, and looked at Laura. "Too much passion, right?"

"No. How is teaching Shakespeare and the classics to adolescent girls satisfying all that fiery passion in you?" Laura placed her hand lightly on Bennie's, resting on the back of the sofa. "Tell me more."

Bennie told Laura about studying directing at Barnard, but how she met her husband in the middle of her freshman year and married him the following June. "Will was eight years older than I. When we married, he wanted to start a family right away. Livie was born on our first anniversary. When she was old enough, I got involved in the community theater group. It's quite good. I direct some and we have visiting directors from New York who are generous with their mentoring. And now I teach drama at Mary Bradford's."

"Why do you say your husband *was* eight years older?"

"I should have said he *is* older. We're separated."

"And your daughter?"

"Staying with Will and his mother for a while, until we get things straightened out."

Laura took her hand away from where it had been resting over Bennie's and sipped her brandy. "I see."

A phone jangled in the bed area and Laura excused herself to answer it. Bennie went to the back glass wall, opaque against the velvet blackness of rural Connecticut. She tried to avoid overhearing the call. Laura's responses were short and without emotion, and she soon hung up. Bennie watched Laura's reflection in the glass as she came back to the sofa. Something about her posture told Bennie the call had upset her.

"Shall I take you back to school?" Laura seemed distracted. She drained her brandy. "You're welcome to stay here and go back tomorrow morning."

Bennie glanced over the low walnut divider to the bed on the other side.

Laura followed her look. "I haven't shown you the guesthouse. There's plenty of privacy, but it's no trouble to drive you back tonight."

"I should go."

"Yes, I'll take you back. On the way you can tell me more about your plans for the drama program."

On the road back to Mary Bradford's, Bennie told Laura about her wish to broaden the drama courses to include more contemporary plays and to increase the number of performances to three a year in addition to the Revel. Laura listened and asked appropriate questions, but she seemed a million miles away. Bennie kept talking to fill the void.

Laura turned off the motor when they pulled up to the residence hall and shifted in her seat to face Bennie. "I hope we'll see each other again. Are you ever in New York? I suppose finding the time would be difficult for you during the week with your teaching responsibilities. Call me if you ever are."

There was a shadow across Laura's face, and her tone was too matter-of-fact to read. She opened her handbag and took out a business card. On the back, she wrote a number. "That's my home phone." She handed the card to Bennie. "Goodbye."

As soon as Bennie was out of the car, Laura started the motor and drove away.

Chapter Ten

New Year's came and went, the girls returned to school, and classes began again. Teachers and students were resigned to living with the long, desolate stretch between the holidays and spring break. Dark, gloomy weather persisted, mirroring Bennie's mood. She called Livie every day but avoided going to see her. She preferred not to share their talks with Olivia.

She often thought of Laura and kept her business card under the edge of the blotter on her desk. She tried to imagine an intersection of their lives that would bring them together again. She fantasized about taking the train into Manhattan and meeting Laura for lunch but hesitated to call, assuming Laura was busy and would resent an intrusion.

During the first week in February, Bennie got a note from Olivia inviting her to supper the following Sunday. The elegant cream-colored note card with Olivia's perfect finishing school handwriting belied her description of a "casual early evening so Livie can be ready for school on Monday." Bennie noticed Olivia ignored that she, Bennie, would have to be ready for school as well. The note was more a summons than an invitation.

Bennie knew what Olivia's agenda was. She wanted to take advantage of Bennie's feelings about all the weeks with little contact with Livie. She wanted to push her toward getting back with Will.

The dinner was Olivia's version of casual. Instead of serving it in the cavernous dining room, Olivia chose to have a table set up in the sunroom in front of bay windows looking over the back gardens, still visible in the gathering twilight. Will was attentive and charming, and Livie kept them entertained, chattering away about her friends at school and how her riding instructor told her Livie and Dasher were becoming a better team every day. Bennie listened hungrily for any hint in her child's excited babble that she had missed seeing her mother.

Bennie chastened herself for being so needy and turned her attention to Will to ask about his business. She knew this tack was a sure-fire way of engaging him. She was surprised when Will deflected her questions back to talk about Livie's riding lessons.

"I'm cutting my time back at work right now. I figure the place can get along without me around for ten hours every day. I like to pick Livie up from school so she's not late for her riding lesson."

Olivia sat quietly, sipping her coffee and watching Bennie's face as she talked with Livie and Will. "It's your bedtime, Livie. Let's go upstairs and I'll read you a story while your mother and father finish their coffee."

"I'd like to put her to bed, Olivia."

Bennie was not there to spend time with Will, and she was sure Olivia knew that well.

"Of course." Olivia nodded.

Livie led the way upstairs. Bennie helped her with her bath and into her pajamas. The steam from the hot water made Livie's blond hair hang in tight ringlets around her face and gave her cheeks a pink glow.

"Mama, will you stay with me 'til I go to sleep? You don't have to read me a story. Scratch my back like you used to do when we were home together, and I know I'll go right to sleep so you don't have to stay too long."

Bennie picked up the little girl, held her in her lap and hugged her.

"Oh, baby. Don't you know how much I miss you and want you with me? Your daddy and I are trying to work out what's best for you, and pretty soon you and I will be together at night like before."

"But Daddy will be staying here, right?" The little girl asked the question matter-of-factly, as though she knew the answer. "Angela's mother and daddy live in two different places too. She has two sets of clothes and toys, but she doesn't have a pony. Dasher would have to live here, right?"

Bennie was unprepared for her child's straightforward questions. She had been selfish, so caught up in her own feelings she failed to think about how all this was affecting her little girl.

"What if you were to stay with me sometimes and here at Grandmother's with Daddy sometimes?"

"That would mean I would be missing someone all the time, either you or Daddy. You don't want him to live with us because you don't like him anymore, right?"

Bennie hugged her again. "Oh, baby, your daddy is a fine person, and he loves you so much."

Bennie had always been careful that Livie not see any unpleasantness between her and Will. She assumed Will had shown the same discretion. Bennie's temper flared as a thought occurred to her. Surely Olivia hadn't been talking to Livie about their separation. Even she wouldn't do that.

"Livie, who told you I don't like Daddy anymore?" Her words were sharper than she'd meant them to be.

The little girl drew back, away from her mother's outburst. "I watch how your face looks when he talks, like you're trying to be polite but not really listening."

Bennie dropped her head, ashamed at how little attention she had been paying to the impact of all this on her child. She hugged her daughter to hide the tears springing to her eyes. There was a subdued knock on the half-closed bedroom door.

"Yes?" Bennie quickly brushed at the tears in her eyes.

Olivia pushed the heavy mahogany door open and stood at the threshold.

"Will and I thought you might want to stay the night with us, for more time with Livie. You're perfectly welcome, of course."

"That's very gracious." Bennie put on the brightest smile she could manage. "But as you know, I have to be back at Mary Bradford's for Monday morning classes."

Will offered to drive Bennie back to school. In the car he continued the conversation about Livie's riding lessons. "I've been thinking of changing riding teachers. I was talking to Jim Lester at the club, and he mentioned a jumping instructor he knows of. I think learning to jump would be great for Livie, good for her confidence. She seems fearless with the pony. What do you think?"

Bennie was sure Will had already made up his mind about the jumping lessons, and that he was going out of his way to make her feel a part of a foregone decision. He offered Bennie a cigarette and lit it for her, then lit one of his own. He glanced at her. "Livie told me you promised to give up smoking."

"I did." She rolled down her window and flicked the cigarette into the dark. "Have you met the instructor?"

"Yes, I have, and she seems to be a cracker jack. She was on the US Olympic team."

"Then you've already arranged it?"

"Well, yes. Do you object?"

Bennie leaned her forehead against the cold glass of the car window. "Are you sure Livie's old enough?"

"Janice, that's the instructor, says so. She's seen Livie ride, and she should know." Will's tone was defensive and belligerent. "Mother thinks it's a fine idea."

"So you've already mentioned jumping lessons to Livie?"

Will gripped the steering wheel. "See, Bennie, these are the kinds of decisions we should be making together. We need to be a family again so that can happen." He steered the car onto the circular drive in front of the residence hall.

Bennie got out without another word and slammed the car door. She watched the car fishtail in the gravel as he sped away. As she walked through the lobby, she absentmindedly glanced at her mailbox. She rarely got mail, but this time there was a piece of paper in her box.

Alice had called only a few minutes earlier and left a message. "Meet me for tea tomorrow afternoon in the village?"

Upstairs, Bennie dialed the number.

Alice answered on the first ring. "I'm glad you called back tonight. You do know 'tea' is code for something with alcohol in it, right?"

Bennie laughed and leaned back against the wall. "In that case, I'm in."

"Good. I have something to talk over with you. What time and where?"

"I can meet you at the Inn in the village at five. What's the mysterious thing you have to talk about?"

"Not mysterious, but important, to me anyway. I'd like to tell you in person."

***

The next day after classes, Bennie bundled up for the walk down the hill to the village. She knotted a red wool scarf around her neck and buttoned up her heavy coat. She crossed the campus, waving to some of her students who were building a snowman in front of the chapel. The Chesterfield Inn dated back to Revolutionary War times, when it was built as a stagecoach stop between Boston and New York. On the wide wooden front porch, she stomped the snow off her boots and entered the tall, double doors.

The bar was almost empty at this early hour, with only a lone bartender in a white apron drying glasses. Alice had arrived before her and had already started on a martini. When Alice noticed Bennie standing in the doorway, her face lit up, and she rushed over to embrace her. Bennie could smell the subtle familiar scent of the expensive perfume Alice had used for years. The smell took her back to times she and Alice shared, especially during their short intimate affair a year before. Bennie held the embrace longer than usual, enjoying the feel of Alice's sturdy body and the muscles of her strong back through her tweed suit coat.

Alice slowly broke the embrace and held Bennie at arm's length, searching her face. "That was awfully nice, but I've a feeling that hug has more to do with what's going on with Will than with me. What is it? What has he done now?"

"Nothing more. It's just that I went to see Livie last night, and she broke my heart asking questions about the reality of what I'm doing to her life. Maybe Will's right. Maybe I'm doing the wrong thing. Maybe it's as Olivia says, a wife and mother must yield to responsibilities and duties."

Alice drew Bennie to a booth in the corner. "Now you listen to me, Bennie. Olivia Grant has never done one thing in her life she didn't find in her own best interest, including trying to make you into a copy of her, and she'll do the same with Livie if she can. Your responsibility is to prevent that for yourself and Livie. You do that by not going back into a marriage with Will on his and Olivia's terms. When would you say no? Where would you draw the line? When would you refuse him? Would you sleep with him? Imagine yourself living with such dishonesty and yet trying to bring Livie up to be her own authentic person. Of course, it's not ideal that you have her only half the time, but time with you will provide a balance so Livie can choose for herself how she wants to be in the world."

"You're right." Bennie patted Alice's hand. "You're such a good friend. But we're supposed to be talking about your news."

"Let me get you a drink first."

Once they were settled with their cocktails, Alice sipped hers and paused for a moment. "I'm thinking of taking a trip. Quite a long trip actually, out to California. The fact is, I'm planning to move there." She rushed on, playing with the olive in her martini and not looking at Bennie. "You remember my college roommate, Bev, right?"

"The architect?" The word made her think of Laura. She shook her head to focus on Alice.

"Yes, she's an architect and she's making quite a name for herself in San Francisco. They've hired her to design the new ballet hall, and she's asked me to come out and live with her. She has a beautiful, big Victorian in Pacific Heights, overlooking the Bay."

Bennie's instinct was to grab the sleeve of Alice's jacket and beg her not to go, not now. She depended on Alice's constant support, taking for granted her friend would always be there with a shoulder to cry on. But she had no rational right to expect that. "San Francisco. Goodness, that seems lovely, such an adventure."

"You make it sound as though I'm headed out to the gold rush. They have come quite a way in a hundred years." Alice turned away and shook her head. "I'd hoped for a different reaction. In my fantasy, my imminent leaving brought you to your senses about us, and you grabbed me and demanded I not go."

Bennie blushed at how close her internal reaction had been to Alice's hope. She grabbed Alice's sleeve, almost knocking her drink over. "Oh, Alice, you are so dear to me, and the only person in the world I can talk to. You've kept me sane through all this, and I can hardly bear to think you'll be gone. You're my closest friend, more than a friend."

"More than a friend and less than a lover? You may be satisfied with that, but it's a real struggle for me. You certainly wanted more when we were together."

"I was so desperately unhappy and so starved for a connection, needing to feel valued as a real person with a brain and an identity."

"And you don't still want that? Is it so easy for you to turn off your feelings for me?"

"The physical part of it, yes, I can turn that off."

"I don't believe that. Remember me? I was there. The first time and all the times we were together. I've never been with anyone more responsive. If I thought there was any way we could go back and that you just need some time…"

Bennie looked at her hands and shook her head. "It's not ever going to happen again, Alice."

Alice raked her fingers through her hair. "My God, I'm on the edge of becoming pathetic here. The truth is through all these months of being just friends, I've been angling for more. I wasn't even serious about California, but now I'll go."

"So you haven't told Bev yet you'll come?" Bennie tried to keep desperate hopefulness out of her voice.

"Not in so many words, but I've probably led her on. I haven't been quite honest with her either about my feelings for you."

They sat in uncomfortable silence, something Bennie couldn't remember happening between them before. She knew Alice was waiting for more from her but offering encouragement would have been self-centered cruelty.

"When will you leave?"

"I've got some financial things to finish up. I need to make sure Mother is going to be okay. Maybe in two or three weeks."

"Two or three weeks? So soon?"

"This has been underway for a while, and Bev is anxious for me to come before she starts the ballet hall project in earnest. I might drive across country and take my time, so that will add a week or ten days." Alice's face brightened. "Why don't you come with me? We can make a sightseeing trip of it, then you can fly back from San Francisco. You could spend some time in Portland. You haven't seen your father in a while, right?"

"You know I have responsibilities here—Livie, not to mention my job, and Town Players starts again in a few weeks." She didn't add her fear Will would use the trip to California with Alice as ammunition in a custody battle.

"It would only be for two weeks or so. You could call Livie every day. Couldn't you get someone to cover your classes and your dorm duty?"

Bennie found the idea of leaving everything behind tempting. "Let me think about it, but I'm sure having me along isn't what Bev has in mind."

Alice hesitated. "You're right. But you let me handle that. You can stay at the Mark Hopkins if you'll be more comfortable."

"I don't think so, but I'll think about it."

"Good." Alice drained the rest of her martini and ate the olive. "I'll take that as a maybe. At least there's a chance. Now tell me all about your dinner date with the impressive Mrs. Clayborn. Isn't that what you called her?"

"I do find her impressive. But before I tell you, you tell me. You left me dangling on the phone the other night about where you met her and under what circumstances. Tell me your story of meeting her before I tell you about our evening."

"I met her at a dinner party in Manhattan, the Upper Eastside, given by two women I know only slightly. They're theater people, an actress and a set designer—quite a chic group of a dozen or so women. You would have fit right in. I was a little out of place, but you know me. I tend to enter a room thinking everyone there is dying to get to know me."

Bennie smiled as she reached across the table and patted her friend's hand.

"Well, after the hostesses had served several rounds of cocktails, it was obvious they were stalling dinner, but we were all having a good time by then, so no harm. Finally, the guest we had been waiting for, Madam Clayborn as it turned out, arrived with a young woman in tow. The hostesses were discreet about it, but they had to hustle and make sure there was a seat at dinner for the unexpected guest. Mrs. Clayborn introduced her as her design assistant, but you wouldn't know that from the conversation. The girl hardly said a word all evening. That's why I made the admittedly catty remark to you on the phone the other night about her liking a different type, young and quiet. That's it. So how was your dinner with the impressive Mrs. Clayborn?"

"It was a success. She plans to make a gift to the drama department at the school. So mission accomplished as far as Mother Berry is concerned. We had dinner at her weekend house in the countryside, just five minutes from here. It was only the two of us...no young quiet girl around that I could tell. Nor any husband in sight. Mother Berry told me she's married to a Broadway producer."

She described the dramatic and remarkable house. "She designed the building herself. It's like a piece of modern art." She wanted her friend to be as impressed with Laura as she was. "She's a good listener. I think I did most of the talking. By the end of the evening, she certainly knew more about me than I did about her. I told her about my directing ambitions. She asked why I'm teaching at Mary Bradford's, and I told her about Will and Livie. Then she drove me back to school."

Bennie left out Laura's offhand invitation to stay the night and the rather mysterious phone call that appeared to change Laura's mood.

"So did she make a pass at you?"

"Alice! The way your mind works."

"Think about it. You might have expected something, but you can be a bit clueless about your impact on other people. Be careful, Bennie."

Alice looked around the room that was filling with the dinner crowd. She pulled on her gloves and gathered her coat and purse.

"Think about the trip to California. If you decide against it, I might fly out after all. Get things moving. I'll let you know."

Bennie took Alice's hand, pulling off the glove her friend had put on, to touch her skin. "Now I could easily become pathetic. Write me, please."

"I will, or I'll certainly call." Alice entwined their fingers. "Take care of yourself, Bennie, and promise you'll be smart about Laura Clayborn."

"I don't have any reason to expect I'll hear from her again, except through her interest in the school."

Chapter Eleven

A tentative knock on her classroom door interrupted Bennie in the middle of a sentence. Miss Dodie opened the door a crack and stuck her head half-way in, mouthing something Bennie couldn't make out. Bennie pushed herself away from the desktop where she had been leaning.

"Read the next scene to yourselves. I'll be right back."

Bennie watched the girls to make sure they had settled into their reading before stepping out of the classroom and closing the door. "What is it?" Bennie looked up and down the deserted hallway.

"Mother Berry sent me to take over your class. She wants to see you in her apartment right away."

"Why?"

"I certainly don't know. You seem to think she confides in me." Miss Dodie shook her head. "I assure you she doesn't."

"Sorry. Have them continue reading the play until the bell."

Bennie hurried down the stairs and out the doors of Barkley Hall. She shivered in the cold wind blowing across the campus. She pictured her warm wool coat, hanging on the back of her desk chair, and regretted rushing away without it. Her feet made crunching sounds on the stubbles of frozen grass as she half-walked, half-ran toward Old Main.

By the time she reached the door to Mother Berry's apartment, she was breathing hard and her nose and cheeks tingled. She took a moment to steady her breathing and covered her face with her thin sweater to try and warm up before knocking on the apartment door. The transom over the door was open, and Bennie could hear Mother Berry in a conversation with another woman. She knocked and heard the clink of a teacup in its saucer and Mother Berry's quick steps to the door before she pulled it open.

"Mrs. Grant, come in. Mrs. Clayborn is here."

"Laura Clayborn?" Bennie looked around Mother Berry into the room.

"Of course, come in and have some tea. Mrs. Clayborn has some very good news for us. I'll let her tell you herself."

Laura stood to face them and peeked around Mother Berry and waved at Bennie with the tea napkin she was holding. "Hello again."

Bennie smiled. "Hello, Mrs. Clayborn."

Mother Berry directed Bennie to sit next to Laura and fussed with pouring her tea. "Mrs. Clayborn has been very complimentary about your ideas for the drama department. She and her husband are going to make a sizable donation to increase the budget for productions and to add more contemporary drama classes for the girls."

Bennie could feel Laura watching her as Mother Berry went on about how much the gift would mean to the school to make sure Mary Bradford's remained "the best, the best, the best."

Laura nodded. "This is a natural for my husband and me with the important part Mary Bradford's played in my life and with Charles's connection to the theater. If things go well, as I expect they will, with your skill as an administrator, Mother Berry, we may consider making our gift ongoing."

Mother Berry's hands flew to her mouth. "Wonderful, wonderful. Just wonderful."

Bennie smiled to herself. Laura certainly knew the way to Mother Berry's heart, praising her beloved school and opening her checkbook.

Laura folded her napkin and picked up her fur coat and purse. "Bennie, will you show me your classroom? You don't mind, do you, Mother Berry? I need to run, but I'd like to be able to describe the current drama program to Charles."

The two women walked back across the campus toward Barkley Hall. "Bennie, would you enjoy seeing *South Pacific* with me in the city next week?"

"You can get tickets for the sold-out Broadway hit of the year?"

Laura smiled and nodded. "The tickets are for Thursday night. Will you be available? Is there someone who can cover your responsibilities here? I would love to see the play with you."

"You surely know you have Mother Berry eating out of your hand. She'd likely sleep in the residence hall herself if she thought it was a request from you. I'd love to see the play with you."

"It's settled then. If you'll take the train in, I'll drive you back after the performance. Can I take a raincheck on seeing your classroom? I'm awfully late. You're going to freeze out here in that sweater." Laura looked around the empty quad area and gathered Bennie to her, wrapping her fur coat around them both. They stood like that for a moment, and Bennie felt Laura's warm breath on her temple.

Laura put her hand lightly against Bennie's face. She gently ran her thumb across Bennie's cheek. "You have the most amazing complexion, like porcelain. I've wondered since the other night at dinner how your skin must feel to the touch. Do you mind?"

Bennie shook her head.

Laura let out a chuckle that started deep in her throat and sent a chill through Bennie.

"Well, I'll see you Thursday then." She turned toward her car.

Chapter Twelve

Bennie climbed down the steps of the train at Grand Central Station and looked up the tracks in the direction of the concourse. No Laura. Bennie had a moment of panic, thinking Laura may have forgotten their date. The engine let out a cloud of steam with a whoosh, and Laura emerged out of the mist, walking toward her and smiling.

"Are you all right to walk to the theater? It's only a few blocks, and traffic's impossible."

Bennie nodded. "Of course."

"That's my girl. We have to hurry." Laura took her arm and guided her through the crowded main concourse of the station, out onto the sidewalk, and across 44th Street to the Majestic Theater.

A crowd of women in furs and men in tuxedos funneled into the lobby. Red SOLD OUT TONIGHT-STANDING ROOM ONLY stickers were plastered across posters of Mary Martin, gazing up adoringly into Ezio Pinza's eyes. The house lights flickered, signaling everyone to find their seats, and Laura guided Bennie through the auditorium door. The usher led them to their row.

"I'll take the seat behind the lady with the big hat," Laura grinned and let Bennie go through to her seat first.

The two of them shared a laugh when the person in front of Laura turned out to be a short, bald man. The orchestra struck up the overture, and Laura took Bennie's hand behind their folded arms, squeezed it, and held on. The closeness felt comfortable and natural to Bennie.

When the final curtain fell, the audience rose in a standing ovation. The actors took their curtain calls, and the lights came up. Bennie leaned toward Laura to be heard over the applause. "Mary Martin was marvelous."

"Yes. Would you like to meet her?"

"What? Now?"

"She arranged the tickets. It'll give us a chance to thank her in person."

Laura took a pen from her purse, wrote a quick note on the back of her business card, and handed the card to the nearest usher. In a minute, he returned to lead them to Miss Martin's dressing room. Bennie stood back as Laura tapped on the door.

Mary Martin, still in makeup and costume, flung the door open and embraced Laura. "Come in, honey." The actress's voice was distinctive and still held the hint of her native Texas. She stood on tiptoes to kiss Laura full on the mouth. "Lolly's here too."

Miss Martin gestured toward a tiny brunette sitting with her legs crossed in the corner of a small sofa. Bennie recognized her as Janet Gaynor, the movie actress. Janet took a drag on her cigarette and made no move to stand up to greet them. "Hello, Laura."

"And who is this one?" Miss Martin smiled at Bennie. She grasped her shoulders, held her at arm's length, and looked her up and down. "She's lovely."

Laura put an arm around Bennie's waist. "This is my new friend Bennie Grant, a budding stage director."

Bennie raised her eyebrows and glanced at Laura. "I'm a drama teacher, hardly a budding anything."

Miss Martin tapped Bennie on the nose. "If you have aspirations toward being a director, it would be an excellent thing, in my opinion. We need more feminine sensibility in this business."

"You were marvelous, Miss Martin. Thank you so much for the tickets."

"You came on a good night. Ezio was at his full-throated best, though I cringe every time he bounds up those stairs in the first act. I'm waiting for him to trip and break a hip at his age." Miss Martin sat down at her dressing table and smeared cold cream on her face. She looked over her shoulder. "Come to dinner with us, Laura."

"Can't make it this time, Mary. I've promised to deliver Bennie back to Connecticut tonight."

"Ah, your place in Connecticut. Lovely." Mary Martin looked from Laura to Bennie in the reflection of the makeup mirror and nodded. "Well, dinner soon then."

After they said their goodbyes, Laura and Bennie left through the stage door. It had begun to rain, and they held hands as they jumped puddles on the way to the parking garage where Laura left her car before meeting Bennie at the train.

Laura steered the car west on 44th Street, toward the Hudson River, then turned north. They rode in silence, and Bennie watched Laura expertly navigate the busy, slippery streets. Laura drove as she seemed to do everything else, with self-assured confidence.

"I love watching you drive."

"What?" Laura glanced over at Bennie, and then back at the road. "I love to drive. I love the feeling of independence and self-determination. One of the best days of my life was the day I could afford to buy my own car."

"When was that?"

"I was nineteen, working at a furniture house on Fourth Avenue as an assistant buyer."

"You didn't go to college?"

"No, my father didn't believe in higher education for girls, so he wasn't about to pay for me. After Mary Bradford's, my choices were to move back to Alabama with him, his new wife, and two little boys, or to find my own way in New York. I decided to get a job and save every nickel to pay for college myself. After two years on the job, my design career was going so well I gave up going to college and used the money to buy a car instead."

Bennie waited, hoping Laura would tell her more. The windshield wipers beat a steady, hypnotic rhythm, and traffic thinned out as they drove farther north. At the Connecticut line, they took the Merritt Parkway toward New Canaan.

It seemed Laura wouldn't volunteer any personal information without being prompted. "How did you come to Mary Bradford's from Alabama?"

Laura glanced at her again. "You want to hear the whole story? I'll warn you, it's sad. Wouldn't you rather talk about the play or about Mary Martin and Janet Gaynor?. You did recognize Lolly was Janet Gaynor, the movie actress, though you may be too young to know who she is. She retired from movies a while ago."

"I did recognize her, and I do want to talk about that, but I think you are in the mood to tell me about yourself, and I'd love to know you better."

Laura was silent for a moment. Bennie thought she might not go on, but then she spoke in an oddly detached voice. "My mother thought she couldn't have a child, though she longed for one. She and my father were in their middle thirties and had been married ten years when I was born. Looking back, I suspect my father resented that I took my mother's time and attention away from him. To give him the benefit of the doubt, he had a difficult life. He was the eldest of eight. His father was a bit of a n'er-do-well, and my father was stuck taking care of his mother and his younger siblings. He gave up his ambition to be a doctor to work the cotton farm beside his brothers.

"My mother was such a kind and gentle person, and she loved me unconditionally. One of my earliest memories is of her weeping as she combed the tangles out of my hair. It was thick even then." Laura paused, cleared her throat, and took a deep breath.

"Here's where the story gets sad. When I was fifteen, my mother got sick with breast cancer, and she died. I couldn't bring myself to go to school for a full year. My father tried making me go, but I couldn't. Finally, he found Mary Bradford's through some of my mother's family who had gone there. I was glad to be away from Alabama and from him, and he was glad to be rid of me. He remarried right away and started a new family."

"Oh, Laura." She put her hand on Laura's knee. She was close to crying, but Laura's stoic expression stopped her. "It makes me feel like crying for you."

Laura glanced at Bennie again. "Here's something funny. My mother told me that when I was a newborn, they kept me in a cradle by their bed. When I cried in the middle of the night, my father startled me into silence by smacking the side of the cradle with a rolled-up newspaper."

"That's not funny. It's horrid."

"Do you think so? It's probably why I seldom cry. Anyway, at first, I went home from school for holidays but with his new wife and his baby twin sons, I was like an outsider. I began staying at school year-round, so that was that. He's gone now."

"What about your half-brothers?"

"I've barely met them. We have no contact. Now you know all about me. Light me a cigarette and find some music on the radio."

Bennie lit two cigarettes and tuned the radio to a station with instrumental music and turned the volume low. She wanted to ask about Laura's husband and about the young woman Laura brought to the dinner party where Alice met her, but she was afraid Laura was on the edge of being impatient with her.

The Parkway was hilly with sharp curves. Trees formed unbroken walls on the shoulder to the right and on the median to the left. Bennie felt claustrophobic in the close quarters of the car's front seat. She rolled the window down a few inches.

"You'll get wet. Let's change the subject. What did you think of the play, from a director's point of view?"

"I'm certainly no expert on directing musical theater." Bennie stopped to sort out her thoughts. "The Rogers and Hammerstein score was the real star of the production. Casting Ezio Pinza, with his operatically trained voice, was a smart move. But the message about racial prejudice…" Bennie's voice trailed off.

"Go on. What about it?"

"I'm thinking about what you said in my room, about my being too intellectual."

Laura chuckled. "I remember. Looking at all your books was a little intimidating. Go on and I'll try to keep up."

"They chose to make the story a romantic comedy, boy meets girl, boy loses girl, boy gets girl back. But it could be about more. On an enchanted evening, two people see each other across a crowded room and have an instant connection. Nellie almost lets prejudice and convention come between them, but love conquers all in the end."

"There's one of your favorite words again, convention. Do you think about what's conventional all the time?"

Bennie heard the question as a rebuke. She turned away from Laura and stared out the window. They had reached New Canaan. Main Street was dark and deserted at the late hour.

"That was harsh on my part. I'm sorry." Laura turned off the radio. "Do you believe in enchanted evenings and instant connections across crowded rooms?"

Her voice was so soft Bennie could barely hear her.

"Oh, yes, but I'm not sure the connections are always mutual."

Laura pulled the car over to the side of the road and stopped without shutting off the motor. She took Bennie's face in both her hands and kissed her tentatively on the mouth. Bennie embraced her and deepened the kiss until Laura pulled away and looked at her with a sly smile.

"I think it's mutual."

Bennie felt a shock of pleasure as Laura's mouth covered hers again and as Laura's hands moved to caress her breasts. Bennie let out an involuntary moan. "Wait. Get us to your house first."

Bennie sat on the edge of the seat, clutching the dashboard, as Laura beat all speed records to the front entrance of her house. She pulled through the gate and alongside the house and stopped the car. "The place will be freezing."

"Come on." Bennie pulled Laura across the seat and out the passenger door. Laura led Bennie into the house and to the bed. They kicked off their shoes and dived under the covers. Laura draped her fur coat over the top of the spread then kissed Bennie's cheeks and blew her warm breath on her nose and ears. She chaffed their hands together to warm them up.

The rain had stopped and moonlight shone through the wall of glass.

Laura unzipped Bennie's dress. She peeled the dress to Bennie's waist and loosened her bra. "I want to see you."

Bennie heard Laura's sharp intake of breath. "Beautiful."

Laura fondled Bennie's breasts and bent her head under the covers to suck them. Bennie's breathing became ragged, and she clutched a handful of Laura's hair. "Don't stop, but aren't you about to smother?"

"Mmm." Laura unzipped her own dress and pressed her naked breasts to Bennie's, rubbing them together, flesh to flesh. Bennie could feel Laura's erect nipples, larger than her own, and hard as pebbles.

Laura whispered in her ear. "You have to tell me what you like."

No one had ever asked Bennie that before. Did Laura want information or did explicit sex talk turned her on? She chided herself to stop thinking and enjoy the sensations her body was feeling. "I'm so aroused that if you touch me right now, I'll come, and I want to make it last longer."

Laura chuckled and pulled Bennie's dress and underpants past her hips and off before taking off her own clothes. They lay facing each other pressed together, breasts, bellies, and thighs.

"Then should I kiss you 'til you come?" Laura gave her deep, soul kisses until they were both breathless. "Or should I do this too?" She rolled Bennie's nipples in her palms. "Too much?"

"No." Bennie took Laura's breasts in her hands and caressed them.

"How about this then?" Laura turned Bennie on her back and traced spirals down her stomach.

Bennie lifted her hips in anticipation of the direction Laura's hand was headed. "Go inside me now." Her voice was a harsh croak.

Laura moved between Bennie's legs, pulling her hips up with one arm and keeping the friction between them until they both climaxed. Laura moved to Bennie's side and stroked her body gently.

"You're trembling."

"I do that," Bennie managed to say.

"So I'm guessing you've been with a woman before. I wasn't sure."

"Yes. I'll tell you, but not now. I want to feel this."

Bennie woke to the delicious aroma of fresh-brewed coffee. Bright sunlight streamed through the glass wall, warming her face. She sat up with a start and bolted out of bed. "Oh my god, what time is it? This is Friday, isn't it? I've got classes."

Laura appeared around the corner of the room divider. She was dressed in a pair of fawn-colored slacks and a chocolate brown cardigan. She had a mug in each hand and a robe draped over her arm. She put the coffee on the bedside table, draped the burgundy silk robe over Bennie's bare shoulders, and pulled her close for a kiss.

"Relax. I called Mother Berry's office and told them we got stuck in the city because of the late hour and the rainstorm. Miss…is the name Dodie or Dobie…will take your classes today."

"It's Dodie. She'll be glad to have the class time, but Mother Berry is going to lose patience with my traipsing around."

Laura arched her eyebrows. "Not as long as it's me you're traipsing with." She sat on the side of the bed, pulled Bennie down beside her, and handed her the steaming mug of coffee. "You owe me the names of the other women you've been with."

"Not women, only one. Funnily enough, you've met her."

"I have? Where? What's her name?"

"Alice Gifford. You met her at a dinner party in the city."

Laura shook her head.

"Hand me my purse. I have her picture."

Laura handed her the bag, and Bennie pulled from her wallet a snapshot of Alice holding the reins of a chestnut horse and smiling for the camera. She showed the photo to Laura.

"You carry her picture?"

"She's my best friend." She ran her thumb over the photo. "Her personality comes through in this."

Laura studied the picture. "I remember her face. Charming, as I recall, and I do remember that night. I'm afraid I wasn't charming that evening. I was dealing with a situation. So you two were lovers? Are lovers?"

Bennie again had the uncomfortable feeling Laura knew more about her than Laura shared about herself. She had a habit of turning the conversation from personal disclosures to questions about Bennie.

"You're a Scorpio, aren't you?"

Laura stared at Bennie. "Why, yes, I am. November 15. How did you know that?"

"You're secretive and brooding." Bennie pulled Laura to her and gave her a long, deep kiss. "And sexy. But before you ask, no, I don't believe in astrology. It was a lucky guess."

"I don't think it's luck. I think you're empathic. I don't mean to be secretive, but the details of a person's life can be complicated and boring. I figure you'll ask me what you want to know, and I'll ask you. So what about Alice Gifford?"

"Alice and I have known each other practically our whole lives. We were lovers but aren't any longer. We have managed to stay best friends."

"Remarkable." Laura looked at the picture again. "I can see the attraction. She's quite attractive."

Bennie expected more questions about Alice and their affair and was surprised when Laura said, "Do you want more coffee or are you ready for me to drive you to school?"

Laura dug under the covers at the foot of the bed and retrieved Bennie's underwear and held up her wrinkled dress.

"I'm afraid this dress will tell a story you may not want your students to know. I have some slacks and a sweater that should fit."

She took the two coffee mugs to the kitchen area.

"You can use the shower here, or would you prefer to run across to the guesthouse?" She came around the corner holding a pair of grey wool slacks and a blue turtleneck with the tags still on them. "See if these will work." She held the sweater next to Bennie's face. "Look how great that shade of blue is with your coloring."

Bennie had heard of keeping a new toothbrush for unexpected overnight guests, but keeping extra outfits was a different matter. Alice's warning about getting involved with Laura came back to her.

As she showered and dressed, Bennie remembered the scene in Mary Martin's dressing room. She wanted to ask Laura about Janet

Gaynor's oddly cool reception as well as Laura's introducing Bennie as a budding director instead of what would have been more accurate, a wife and mother marking time as a drama teacher in a girls' school and a jack-of-all-trades in a community theater. Bennie supposed those characterizations wouldn't interest Mary Martin and Janet Gaynor.

She came out of the bathroom toweling dry her short hair.

Laura was in the kitchen buttering bread. "I'm making us some toast."

"I see you are. Laura, did you mean what you said about me asking you what I want to know about your life and your thoughts?"

"I try to always mean what I say." Laura put the knife down and waited. "Last night, in Mary Martin's dressing room, you introduced me as a budding director. What were you thinking?"

"That's how I see you. It's what you aspire to be, isn't it? In fact, I'm not sure I understand why you're marching in place instead of getting on with your life. Do you need the money from this teaching job?"

"No, but I have to focus on getting custody of my child." Bennie felt Laura was judging her, and she hated that she needed to defend her choices. "I owe Mother Berry for coming to my rescue with a job and a place to live on very short notice."

Laura laughed a short, barking laugh. "Believe me, that old war horse wouldn't do you any favors that don't benefit her precious school. Besides, you brought in Charles's and my gift. I'd say you've paid your debt to Mother Berry." She picked up the knife and went back to buttering the toast. "What else do you want to ask me?"

Bennie wanted to ask about Mary Martin, and the young woman Laura had brought to the dinner party where Alice met her, and her marriage to the Broadway producer, and what last night had meant, but she suspected those questions would be beyond some kind of boundary.

"Nothing more."

Chapter Thirteen

Ever since Alice proposed they drive to California, Bennie tried to think how she might justify being away from the school and Livie. She decided the risk was too great. Will would take the trip as evidence she and Alice were still involved, even if Mother Berry approved her absence. She reluctantly told Alice it wouldn't work.

Alice booked an overnight flight from LaGuardia to San Francisco and Bennie rode the train to the airport with her to see her off.

"They call this a red-eye flight, for the obvious reason that I'll probably look like hell at the end of it. I hope I don't scare Bev to death when she picks me up at the airport." Alice took her ticket out of her purse to check the gate number again.

As they walked down the airport concourse toward Alice's gate, Bennie eyed the fur coat Alice wore around her shoulders. "Are you taking that fur with you to California?"

"San Francisco is colder in spring than New York. Besides, I imagine we'll be going to lots of ballets and operas. It's a small town with big culture, and I suspect all us ladies will be in our furs."

Alice stopped in the middle of the hallway. People rushed past them in both directions. Alice put her hands on Bennie's shoulders. "If you want to change your mind and come out for a few days or even longer, call me. You know what a bad letter writer I am, but I'll be thinking about you. Take care of yourself, and don't do anything rash while you're waiting to be settled with Will."

Bennie shook her head and lowered her gaze from Alice's open and trusting face. She hadn't confessed to Alice anything about the night with Laura. She told herself it was because Alice would worry about something she could do nothing about. But if she were honest with herself, she knew Alice was right that getting involved with Laura could potentially give Will and his mother ammunition in a custody fight. Bennie was embarrassed by her inability to resist Laura.

***

Alice read Bennie's mind. "Bennie." She tilted Bennie's chin up to look directly into her eyes. "Do yourself a big favor. Don't get involved with her. You know Will would use your involvement with her against you. If you already are involved, it's way too late for me to do anything but lecture you, and I don't want that to be our parting memory. Be careful. Let's say goodbye here."

Bennie watched her walk quickly away. She waited for Alice to turn for a last wave, but she headed straight down the concourse and disappeared around a corner.

Because of the late hour on the train back to New Canaan, there were only a dozen other passengers, most of them dozing in the darkened car. Bennie stared out at the grey shapes of apartment buildings. The train occasionally passed lighted windows, so close that Bennie had the sensation of leafing through pictures in a stranger's photograph album—a woman leaning over the stove to light a cigarette, a bald man in his tee shirt at a kitchen table, a woman washing dishes.

In the dark, swaying train coach, Bennie promised herself she would take Alice's advice against becoming any more involved with Laura. She determined to concentrate on getting through the few weeks until spring break and seeing Livie as often as possible. Livie had started her jumping lessons, and Bennie was interested in meeting the new riding instructor Will was so high on.

***

The smells of the riding arena—sawdust, hay, and freshly-applied paint—mixed with the spring smells of the woods around the Grant mansion. Bennie leaned on the top fence rail, watching the new riding instructor lead Dasher, with Livie on his back, around the circle at a trot. She was impressed with the instructor's competence. She seemed patient but firm. What Will hadn't said was that she was very attractive too.

Bennie judged she and the instructor were about the same age, late twenties. The instructor's long dark hair was tied back at the nape of her neck in a ponytail that bounced as she ran alongside Dasher and Livie. The sleeves of her white cotton shirt were rolled up, showing tanned, sinewy forearms, and her jodhpurs and calf-high boots showed off her figure, toned by hours of riding horses and running alongside her students.

Every few feet, poles lay on the ground so that the pony had to learn to time his gait to step over them, then recover and prepare for the next pole. Bennie knew this was the first phase in teaching Livie and her horse to jump. Pride swelled in her breast at her daughter's apparent fearlessness. The instructor was constantly correcting and encouraging both the pony and the rider, telling Livie, "Hands forward. Keep the reins slack. Hold on to his mane when he steps over the pole. Good."

Bennie was tempted to shout her own words of encouragement but held herself in check for fear of breaking Livie's concentration. As it was, she noticed Livie steal a peek in her direction each time they passed, so she restrained herself to a nod and an encouraging smile.

"Bring him into the center and walk him back and forth down the long line to let him cool off," the instructor coached Livie. "Don't let him trot. That's it."

When the instructor seemed confident Livie and Dasher were settling into the cool-down phase of the lesson, she turned, removed her gloves, and stuffed them into her back pocket. She walked over to Bennie with her hand extended. "You must be Mrs. Grant."

"Yes, I'm Bennie Grant. Please call me Bennie."

"Janice Traynor." The woman's hand was slender, but her handshake was firm and confident. She was almost as tall as Bennie.

"Your name is your destiny." Bennie laughed even as she regretted the cliché the woman must have heard a thousand times.

"Yes. The spelling is with a 'y' and 'o.' The good thing is it's easy for my clients to remember."

"So jumping is your specialty."

"Teaching it is, yes. This is our third session. I hope you can tell how well Livie's doing. She's a natural."

"Mr. Grant thought she would be."

"Well, it's nice to meet you, Bennie. Livie and I need to brush, feed, and water Dasher. Please come by our lessons often. I can see Livie enjoys showing you how well she's doing."

"I will."

Janice drew on her gloves, and Bennie noticed a thin white gold ring on her left ring finger.

"There's Mr. Grant now. I'll go help Livie dismount. She'll want to tell him all about her lesson."

Will came rushing down the brick pathway from the house. He waved to Bennie and went straight to where Janice was helping Livie down from her pony. "I'm sorry I missed the lesson. Huge pile-up on the Parkway. How did she do today? How was it, honey?" He bent down on one knee to speak to Livie despite the sawdust and dirt.

Bennie leaned against the fence with her chin resting on her hand. She watched Livie describe to her father what she and Dasher had learned, complete with running to a pole and stepping over it to demonstrate Dasher's part. Janice stood to the side, smiling and nodding.

Will looked at his watch and then at Janice. "I'm keeping you past time. I'll definitely be here next week to watch the whole lesson." He shook hands with the instructor and watched as Janice and Livie led Dasher into the stables. He turned to head across the arena toward Bennie and noticed for the first time he was up almost to the tops of his Italian leather shoes in loose dirt and sawdust. Bennie smiled as she watched him hold his pant legs up and high step toward the fence. She knew how particular he was about his shoes.

"Bennie, come up to the house. I'll see if I can get us some lemonade while Livie finishes up. Or something stronger if you prefer. It'll give us a chance to talk."

They walked up the brick path to a terrace that offered a view of the stables and the woods behind.

They settled with their lemonade. "So you carried through with starting Livie learning to jump."

"Yes, Janice says she has a real knack for it. I suspected she would." Will smiled and nodded. "Janice has turned out to be the right instructor for Livie. We were lucky to get her."

"She seems very competent."

"Yes, well." Will sipped his drink and Bennie waited for him to start whatever talk he had in mind. She kept an eye on the stables, wishing for Livie to finish quickly.

"I heard at the club that Alice went to California."

"Yes, to San Francisco."

"Is she out there for good? San Francisco might be the best place for her."

His question violated both Alice's privacy and her own. She could imagine the idle speculation going on back and forth among Will's friends over afternoon cocktails beside the tennis courts. Do these people have nothing better to do with their time? "Her plans are not firm right now."

"Does her leaving have anything to do with you?"

Bennie's anger flared. "Will, please don't try and draw me into whatever soap opera you and your crowd are scripting for Alice. She's my friend. I would expect you to have the decency and discretion to avoid such gossip about the mother of your child."

"Hold on now, Bennie. I'm not asking out of idle curiosity." He placed his drink on the glass-topped table. His normally pink complexion turned a deeper shade, and Bennie knew she had struck a nerve. "A condition of our six-month agreement about Livie is that you assure me things are over with Alice. I'm asking if I can take her leaving as a positive sign of that?"

"I won't talk about Alice with you, Will."

"All right, all right." He held his hands up in a conciliatory gesture. "I'm just saying, these last months have been pleasant enough between us, don't you agree? You can see how happy Livie is when we're all together. Aren't you ready to move on?"

"What do you mean move on?"

"Move beyond this. Put all this behind us." He rushed on as Bennie turned away. "Let's move back into our house." He reached across the table and took her hand in both of his. "Look, I'm a realist. My expectations aren't high about anything between you and me, but we can be a family again, can't we?"

Bennie turned back and saw in his face the image of the confident young man she had married, one whose expectations didn't have to be lowered. She felt a deep sadness for all of them—herself, Will, and Livie.

"No, Will, you know we can't. I can't." Tears welled up in her eyes.

He dropped her hand and pulled a white linen handkerchief from his pocket and offered it to her. His lips took on the all-too-familiar exasperated tight, straight line. "Is that your final decision, Bennie?"

She nodded.

"Then I guess that's that."

Bennie looked up in surprise. Had he finally accepted the inevitable? "Can we file the divorce papers now?"

"Oh, no. We still have months to go on our deal. Mother and I are in total agreement on this. She's a real trooper, stepping up to take Livie and me in, and you and I made a deal."

Will might be ready to give up the idea of putting their marriage back together, but his mother wasn't. She shook her head, ready to confront the issue, when the click of riding boots coming up the brick walk and Livie's excited chatter interrupted.

Bennie rose and walked into the house. She stood just inside the French doors while she composed herself. She wanted to keep as much of this as possible away from Livie. She watched Will stand and smile, chatting with the instructor, relaxed with his hands in his pockets. It dawned on her that Will was attracted to Janice Traynor, and the purpose of their conversation was to give Bennie another chance to come back into the marriage before pursuing a relationship with the riding instructor. Behind her, Bennie heard the unmistakable cadence of Olivia's footsteps.

"Bennie, why are you standing here in the doorway? Aren't you and Will having a lemonade?" Olivia glanced through the glass toward Janice and Will. The two women watched them exchange a few more words before Janice took off her riding gloves and offered her hand, her manner very professional. Janice patted Livie on the head and strode down the brick path toward the barn.

"You must have met Livie's new riding instructor. She's very graceful, isn't she?"

Olivia was so transparent, Bennie could have slapped her. "I suppose that comes from spending significant time astride a thousand-pound animal."

Olivia looked at Bennie with a slight smile and nod. "I'll let you and Will get back to your drinks."

"Oh, we're finished. I'll just take Livie up for her bath."

Chapter Fourteen

One evening three weeks later, after dinner in the residence dining hall, Bennie found a light blue envelope in her mailbox. Her address was written in Alice's familiar bold hand and had a return address in San Francisco. She tore the envelope open eagerly and a photograph fluttered to the floor. It was a picture of Alice in sunglasses, standing on a terrace or balcony, the wind whipping her hair. Behind her in the distance were the Golden Gate Bridge and San Francisco Bay.

Bennie stood in the lobby in front of the mailboxes reading the letter.

Dearest One,

I know you'll forgive me for not having written before now, since you could hardly expect I'd change old habits. And I'll admit I've hesitated to write because I'm afraid you might feel upset with me for the way we parted. I was unjustifiably preachy about Laura Clayborn. Please forgive me if you are angry.

Enough mea culpa. *San Francisco really is a small town. Everyone knows everyone's business, and the favorite pastime is justifying how they're just as good as New York and so much better than Los Angeles. Makes one want to go to Los Angeles to see how the barbarians down there live. San Francisco (never say Frisco!) is only about one hundred years old, and the founding fathers were failed gold prospectors who found selling picks and shovels to the other prospectors a more reliable way to a fortune. How's that for a quick history lesson? I won't deny there is a certain upstart charm to the place. Bev would never have gotten the professional opportunities she has here in San Francisco if we were in New York or even Chicago.*

About Bev. She works night and day on the ballet hall. Being chosen for this project is an incredible distinction. Another thing about San Franciscans, they take their culture seriously. Did you know they had the first professional ballet company in the country? Anyway, Bev's quite a star around town, and we get invited to all the best parties. Both of us get invited since it's assumed we're a couple. Not spoken aloud, of course. She has a smart circle of friends, both men and women, including more traditional relationships, and they've accepted me graciously.

I think of you every day. As I calculate, you've only two more months until the end of your "deal with the devil." If you need a distraction, the invitation still stands for a visit to California if you could somehow find time away from the school. Turns out Bev would be fine with your coming. She's not the insecure type, and, as I said, consumed right now with her work. You and I would have tons of free time to explore the city. It's really quite charming. Please keep it in mind.

You know, all my love, Alice

Bennie held the letter to her face and smelled Alice's familiar fragrance. How much easier these last weeks would go if she could spend time with Alice. A trip would give a welcome diversion from Olivia's pressure for reconciliation. If there was any way in the world she could take time off from teaching, she could still call Livie every day to hear about school and her jumping lessons. Two weeks would be a long enough visit to give her some relief and make the time until June 24th seem to go faster.

The more she thought about the invitation, the more excited she grew. She ran up the stairs two at a time, pulled some stationery from her desk, and settled on her bed to write Alice.

Dear, dear Alice,

You always seem to come through as my savior at the right moment. I just got your letter, and it couldn't have come at a better time. You must have picked up my vibrations. This waiting for the end of June seems interminable. It appears Will has finally dropped the notion that I'll give up on the divorce, but Olivia hasn't, so he's determined to run the whole course. I'm living from week to week.

Far from being angry with you about the way we parted, I'm grateful for your voice of reason. I know you're only looking out for me. Your advice came at the most opportune time. I won't say anything more until I can see you in person. Which brings me to your invitation.

San Francisco sounds delightful. I have visited there. One summer my father and I took a short sightseeing trip there, but I was only ten or so. The city would be entirely different now, and seeing it with you would be the best. Could I really run away from everything that's unpleasant and unsettled here to visit you for two weeks or so? As far as Livie's concerned, I'm sure she would be fine with phone calls every day. The school term ends in three weeks, and I've decided to give Mother Berry notice I won't be coming back in the fall. Things will be settled by then, and it's time for me to stop marching in place.

Olivia would disapprove of my coming, of course, since she values every opportunity to get us together as a family. She'll stir Will up about it. Still, I'm tempted. Call me when you get this letter and ask me one more time, and I think that will do the trick.

I miss you, Bennie

Bennie sealed and stamped the envelope, and after classes the next day, she headed down the hill to the post office in the village. It seemed all seventeen thousand New Canaan residents decided to occupy the same four block-long downtown area at the same time. The post office sat in the middle of a block, wedged between Essie's Tearoom and Tipton's Hardware.

In the small lobby of the post office, a long line of customers snaked around itself. Bennie located the outgoing mail slot, relieved that she had stamped Alice's letter at home and didn't have to stand in line. She hesitated only a moment before dropping it in and listening for the rustle of the letter falling into a canvas bag of outgoing mail. She never completely trusted her letter wouldn't get stuck in the slot.

At the door, there was an awkward moment when a man tried to tip his hat, balance a package, and hold the door for her all at the same time. She heard her name being called from behind her in the line of waiting customers.

"Mrs. Grant. Bennie." She turned to see an attractive young woman smiling at her. "It's me, Janice Traynor. I know I look different away from the barn."

The riding instructor stepped out of line and offered her hand. Her long hair was loose instead of pulled back in a ponytail, and she wore a white silk shirt and black slacks in place of the cotton shirt and jodhpurs she wore for teaching. "Livie and I have missed you. We thought you might come again to watch our lessons."

"Oh, I don't want to distract her, and the jumping lessons are Will's thing. He's giving up time at the office to encourage her, so I've stayed away. Will's coming faithfully, I hope." Bennie didn't say was she was glad to have Will spend time with Janice without her around, and she hoped their relationship would move beyond employer and employee.

"Oh, yes. He never misses."

"Well, I won't keep you from your business." Bennie gestured toward the long line of customers.

"I'm just picking up stamps. It's kind of silly to be doing that at a busy time like this. I've got a rare free afternoon, so I'm getting to know downtown New Canaan a little better. It's so nice to run into you like this. Would you like to have a cup of coffee or tea? If you have time, that is."

Bennie wanted to decline, but Janice seemed eager, and Bennie couldn't find an excuse. They went next door to the tearoom and found a sunny table for two near the front window.

They both ordered tea from the waitress, who was so young and flustered that Bennie thought she must be a high school girl working part time. The girl finally got their orders correct and left the two women sharing an awkward silence. When they both began talking at once, Janice laughed. "You go first."

"You said you're getting to know New Canaan. Did you just move here?"

"Yes, around the time I started working with Livie. Before that I taught riding at Brunswick Academy and lived on campus there."

"Is your family here with you?"

"No, it's just me." Janice followed Bennie's gaze to the band on her left hand. "Oh, you mean this." Janice held up her finger. "The wedding ring was my mother's. I've gotten in the habit of wearing it for convenience. There are certain kinds of men in my business who see women who ride as Valkyrie figures. They're attracted by the prospect of taming our warrior natures. I find the ring effective for discouraging unwanted attention."

"Aren't you afraid you'll discourage the other kind, the wanted attention?"

Janice smiled. "I haven't found that to be a problem."

"I suspect not." Bennie silently hoped Janice welcomed Will's attention.

"But what about you? I noticed when you visited our lessons you weren't coming from the house, and you're not wearing a wedding ring. I hope I'm not out of line."

"No." Bennie looked at the emerald engagement ring on her left hand. She stopped wearing her wedding band when she and Will separated. "Will and I are divorcing. He and Livie are staying with his mother for a few months until we get things sorted out."

"I see." Janice nodded as though Bennie's disclosure answered several questions for her.

After the waitress brought their tea, they sat in silence a moment, the only sound the clinking of their spoons on China while they stirred their tea. Bennie was relieved to change the subject.

"If I'm not out of line, as you say, what made you decide to leave Brunswick this close to the end of the term?"

Janice sipped her tea before answering. "It's a long story." She looked out the window. "But believe me, my leaving had nothing to do with teaching or my students. I'll just say Brunswick is probably a bit too provincial to be a good match for me."

"Let's hope New Canaan provides a better match. I appreciate your work with Livie. I know Will feels the same."

"She's a pleasure."

When she finished her tea, Bennie pushed away from the table. "Well, I must be off, and you have to get your stamps." She reached for the bill, but Janice was quicker.

"It was my invitation."

They stopped on the sidewalk in front of the tea shop. The crowds were a little thinner, but seemed more frenetic, hurrying to finish their business and get home. Janice put a hand on Bennie's elbow and steered her closer to the building, out of the flow of foot traffic. The gesture took Bennie by surprise, a bit awkwardly familiar, but not exactly unpleasant.

Bennie extended her hand. "Thank you for tea. I enjoyed our conversation. We must do it again some time."

"Did you? I hope so. Maybe you'd be my tour guide around some of the historic sites of New Canaan. I'm generally free on Fridays."

"We'll definitely do that. I may be out of town for a few days, but after that. Well, you'd better get those stamps. The window will close soon. Goodbye, Janice."

Chapter Fifteen

Days went by without a call from Laura. Bennie was relieved that her resolve not to see Laura wasn't being tested, but she thought about her every day and kept Laura's business card in the corner of her blotter. She was tempted to call the number in New York, but so far she had resisted. She pictured Laura going about her life in the city, thinking about her too. She was oddly certain Laura would contact her. She just wasn't sure what she would do when it happened.

After mailing her letter to Alice, Bennie had time to think of all the problems that could arise if she followed through on her visit to San Francisco. She knew Will would be dead-set against it. He would take her going to see Alice as backsliding and might threaten her again with losing Livie for good. Olivia would certainly only make matters worse. She wouldn't want Bennie to escape the last few weeks of her attempts to encourage reconciliation. By the time Alice called, Bennie had decided against going to San Francisco.

"Why? Your letter sounded so encouraging."

"Do you really want me to go through all the dreary reasons? I'm depressed enough."

"I can hear you're on edge. Tell me the dreary reasons."

"You know how Will and Olivia would react to an announcement that I'm going to California to see you."

"Don't tell them."

"Alice, I can't just disappear."

"Tell them you're going to Portland to visit your father. You can take a few days and fly up to see him, so it wouldn't be a lie, not exactly anyway, and you can call Livie every day."

Bennie hesitated.

"Is it about Laura Clayborn? You hinted in your letter there was more to be said about that. Are you involved with her?"

"You know I can't talk about some things on this phone. But I'll say I haven't seen or heard from her in several weeks."

"If it is her, you can bring her with you, you know. We'd be just one big happy foursome. You can stay at the Mark Hopkins if you'd be more comfortable."

"You know what I'm facing here with Will and his mother. I don't see how I can make a trip to California work. You're a dear for offering. Will you ask me again once this is over?"

"Of course."

Laura called the following week. The message in Bennie's box read *Call me at the New York number.* Bennie waited until the girls settled into their rooms after dinner before making the call. She was prepared to decline an invitation with the excuse of end of school year duties, but she was unprepared for the shock of pleasure the sound of Laura's voice stirred in her.

"Laura, it's Bennie."

"Bennie, you'll never believe who called my husband. I won't keep you in suspense. Will called Charles."

Bennie's knees went weak, and she leaned against the wall of the tiny phone alcove to keep her balance.

"Why? What did he want?"

"That's the funny thing. He's the president of the country club or the chairman of the membership committee or something like that. He heard of our gift to the school and my house in New Canaan, and he's giving us the rush to join the club. Charles handed the phone to me." Laura chuckled. "Charles isn't the athletic type, and he's hardly ever been to New Canaan. Anyway, your husband invited me to go by the club. He's sure I'll be impressed. Isn't that delicious irony?"

Bennie let out a sigh of relief. One of the girls had taken the chair that usually sat in the tiny phone booth so Bennie slid down the wall to sit cross-legged on the floor.

"Hello? Are you still there?"

"I'm here."

"I thought you and I might go there for a game of tennis this weekend. Do you play tennis? I don't even know."

"I played on the tennis team at Mary Bradford's and in my freshman year at Barnard, but that doesn't say much. Neither team was very good."

"Great, we'll be well-matched. I thought you might like to come to the house for supper afterward. I promise the place won't be as cold as last time."

Anyone listening to the conversation would have missed Laura's subtle insinuating tone, but her voice struck Bennie like an electric jolt. She struggled to find the right words to resolve the conflict between her physical response to Laura and her resolve to avoid the danger of involvement with her. Bennie closed her eyes and rubbed her hand across the front of her shirt, as if she could calm her racing heart.

"Things are chaos here the last two weeks of school. The girls are already starting to pack. Just getting all the gowns out of the formal closet is a major project. My floor is all seniors, so they have to prepare for graduation." Bennie heard herself rattling on and on. She stopped and took a breath. "I really should say no this time."

"Oh." Laura sounded surprised. "Of course. I understand. I've been frantically busy myself. I've taken on a hotel project, the biggest of my career, and one of my design assistants quit without notice."

Bennie wondered if the design assistant who quit was the young woman Laura brought to the dinner party where Alice met her.

"Well, another time then. Goodbye."

"Goodbye."

Bennie hung up but left her hand on the receiver. She looked at the business card with Laura's home number written on the back. She picked up the phone and dialed the number again.

Laura answered on the first ring.

"You should go see the club. It's quite lovely, and they're famous for the quality of their clay tennis courts. I could spare enough time for a few games."

Laura chuckled. "Good. I'll pick you up at eleven tomorrow."

Chapter Sixteen

Laura and Bennie turned onto the access road for the New Canaan Country Club. At first, they could just see the top of a flagpole with the American flag waving in the stout breeze. As the car climbed higher, the stately Norman-style clubhouse came into view. A large round tower and portico dominated its red brick edifice. Huge arched windows ran across the first floor, and dormers lined the second-floor rooftop.

Laura whistled. "Impressive, but it doesn't look like a place to have fun."

"It's a bit stuffy. That's the way the members like it. They tried to make the clubhouse look like a castle in Northern France."

"I can see that."

Bennie led Laura through the heavy double front doors and stopped at a reception area just inside. The woman at the desk looked up from her logbook and put on the glasses hanging from a chain around her neck. "Mrs. Grant. How lovely to see you. We have both of you today."

Bennie froze, her hand poised over the logbook.

"Yes, both you and Mrs. Grant Senior. She's having lunch with us."

Bennie nodded, shooting Laura a look. "Nice to see you too, Ina. This is my guest and a potential new member, Mrs. Charles Clayborn."

Bennie wrote Laura's name in the logbook and led her through the carpeted foyer and down a hallway lined with lighted display cabinets full of photographs of tennis and golf players and silver trophies dating from the beginning of the club in the early 1900s.

They changed into tennis clothes in the ladies' dressing room, which looked more like a boudoir than a locker room. It was decorated in pastel colors with over-stuffed chairs and ottomans upholstered in chintz fabric. Instead of metal lockers for their street clothes, there were white French Provincial cabinets. A vanity mirror ran along one wall with four upholstered stools in matching chintz.

Laura fingered the material on one of the chairs. "This place gives me the creeps. It could use an update. If I joined, do you think they'd let me redecorate?"

"I doubt it since the ladies steering committee just finished a year-long re-do. This is how they like it."

Outside, the full spring sun made the freshly groomed, bright orange clay tennis courts appear unreal, as though they were drawings in a comic book.

Bennie led the way onto the court. "Looks like we have the place to ourselves this morning."

After they warmed up, Bennie had the first serve. She took some speed off her strokes and stayed at the baseline, feeling out the pace that would make Laura comfortable. After a long rally, though, Laura followed a backhand to the net for a winner.

Bennie blew out a breath. "Oh ho, that's the way it's going to be, eh?"

They began to compete in earnest, Bennie's conservative, steady game contrasting with Laura's risk-taking style of play. In the end, Laura took three out of five sets. Bennie bent over to catch her breath.

"That's it for me. I need to quit while I'm behind. Let's find a place to have some iced tea."

They chose a quiet table by the Olympic-sized swimming pool, still bearing its plastic shroud from winter. Bennie caught the eye of a waiter, and he hurried over. "Can you bring us iced teas?"

"Of course, Mrs. Grant. Right away."

Laura smiled as the waiter sprinted away from their table.

"What's so funny?"

"I was thinking about how second nature all this seems to you." Laura made a three-hundred-and-sixty-degree gesture taking in the tennis courts, pool, busy lunch tables, golf course in the distance, and the stately club house. "I've always been too busy with my business to think about joining a country club, but I can see the attraction. What happens when you're divorced? Do you and your husband get joint custody of the country club membership?"

"No. Divorced men can be members but not divorced women. He'll keep the membership. They made that rule so as not to disturb the tranquility they've worked so hard to create here."

"That doesn't seem quite fair."

"I don't care. He can have it."

Laura took a cigarette from her bag and offered one to Bennie. "Have you thought about what you'll do once you're divorced? If you want to pursue your directing ambitions, Charles can certainly open doors on Broadway for a director's assistant job."

"If all goes well, and Will lives up to his promise, I'll have Livie regularly."

"What has he promised?"

Bennie told her about their meeting on Christmas Eve. "I had to swear things were off with Alice and that I would not expose Livie to what he calls my odd leanings."

Laura shook her head. "I see how you can live up to the technical terms of such an agreement, but Will surely isn't so naive as to think Alice is the only person you might become involved with."

"He sees it as a one-time aberration with Alice only. I honestly don't think he attaches much significance to the affair. He said as much." She blew out a cloud of smoke that broke up in the light breeze. "But he doesn't hesitate to use it to threaten me."

A mixed foursome had taken over one of the tennis courts. They played with skill and were well-matched. The steady pock-pock sound of their long rallies drifted across to the two women.

Laura leaned toward Bennie. "About going back with him, don't you worry that might be worse for your child than a divorce? Living with a mother who is forced to deny her own nature may not be the best upbringing for a little girl."

Bennie turned away from Laura and rubbed her temples. "Of course, I worry about that."

"I think you'd like to say I'm not a mother and I can't understand. It's true I seem to have no sign of maternal instinct. I've known this all my life. But I see the struggle you're going through, and I'm not a person who's completely without empathy. I may see it more objectively than you, that's all. If you want me to stay out of it, I will."

Bennie pressed her knee against Laura's under the table. "I appreciate your concern." She searched for words to move the spotlight off her troubles. "Haven't you ever wanted children? Hasn't your husband?"

"You must have noticed Charles and I don't have what you might call a traditional marriage. We found each other early in our careers, and at the time a marriage was convenient for both of us and has stayed so for twenty years."

"How were you so sure, about having children I mean?"

"You're always interested in my life story, so here's a chapter. I told you about growing up in Alabama. My mother and father and I, and all my father's family, went to the First Baptist Church every Sunday morning and Sunday evening. Sunday morning at ten o'clock was Sunday School, then a break, then the sermon at eleven. We never missed. The ritual was as rigid as any you read about in history, the Druids, the Greeks, the Romans. Any of it.

"After Sunday School, the men gathered on the grass outside the front door of the church to smoke and joke with each other. They all wore their Sunday suits with white shirts buttoned up to the top and their hair slicked back. They looked so different from the men they were during the week, farmers and mill workers and merchants with care-worn faces. For those few minutes, they left worries behind and enjoyed being with each other. The women, on the other hand, spent the time after Sunday School in the nursery, settling babies who were too young to sit through the sermon, or they worked in the church kitchen preparing for some fellowship event after church. In other words, doing the things they did every day of their lives.

"My earliest memories are of rejecting the idea of being stuck in a subservient role, and those women with children painted that picture in my mind early on. Symbolically, I wanted to be one of those men standing outside the church on the lawn instead of stuck in the nursery or the kitchen. That's a much longer answer than the question warranted. There's even more to the story, if you want me to go on." Laura sipped her tea.

"Please." Bennie noticed again the detached tone of Laura's voice.

"One Sunday morning in the summertime, when I was fourteen or so, Mother let me sleep late and skip Sunday School on my promise to get myself ready and walk the half mile from our farm to the church in time for the sermon. As I trudged up the gravel road toward the front of the church, kicking rocks and not caring if they scuffed my Sunday shoes, I noticed the usual cluster of men. My father was one of them, and in the middle was the most beautiful woman I had ever seen. She was tall, the same height as most of the men, and she was perfectly at ease interacting with them. I was thunderstruck. It was the first time I had encountered a woman who broke the mold, defied the stereotype.

"It was love at first sight. She turned out to be a new teacher in our high school. She lived on her own and drove an automobile. She seemed to me to be able to make her own decisions and be who she wanted to be. I had a huge crush on her the whole next year. The following summer, she moved on."

Bennie thought of the first time she saw Laura, encircled by men at the board reception. She had been attracted by the same presence in Laura, perfectly comfortable in the situation, not typical of a woman's traditional role.

"So here's the punchline, finally. A few years ago, I hired someone to find her, and I telephoned her. I'm not sure what I expected or wanted. To tell her what she meant in the life of that thirteen-year-old girl, I suppose. She was living in Birmingham, a widow with three grown children. When I asked if she remembered that summer morning in front of the church she said no, but she did remember the feeling of being in a new town and not knowing the customs. She stood out in front of the church with the men that morning because she didn't know any better. Isn't that funny?"

Before Bennie could respond, Laura's eyes shifted from Bennie's face to beyond her left shoulder.

"Don't look now." Laura barely moved her lips. "There's a woman making a beeline for us, and if you were the director of this play, and you were casting the role of your mother-in-law, she'd win hands-down."

Bennie fixed a smile on her face as she stood and turned to watch Olivia walk toward their table.

"Hello, Bennie. Getting in some early spring tennis, I see." Olivia's gaze subtly shifted to take in Laura from head to toe.

Laura stood and extended her hand. "You must be Olivia Grant. I've heard so much about you from Bennie. I'm Laura Clayborn."

"Ah, yes. On the board at Mary Bradford's." She took Laura's hand. "My son mentioned you might give our little club a tryout. How pleasantly surprising to see you here with Bennie."

"I enlisted her." Laura's fingers lightly touched the small of Bennie's back. "I'm not that familiar with country clubs."

Olivia gestured toward the tennis courts. "You know your way around a court, I noticed. High risk and high reward appear to be your game."

"Thank you for the compliment, but I don't fool myself that I'm good for the long run. More a flash-in-the-pan."

"Yes, well. Are you having lunch, Bennie? Will and Janice took Livie to a horse show today, so I'm footloose."

Bennie noticed Olivia's familiar use of the instructor's first name, so atypical of Olivia's usual attitude toward the hired help. Olivia was still hoping to make her jealous.

Olivia nodded toward a table where two of her friends sat watching the exchange. They waved in Bennie's direction. "Will you join us?"

Bennie glanced at Laura. Did she feel as serene as she looked? If so, she would be perfectly at ease spending an hour being sized up by Olivia.

Bennie shook her head. "I think we'll finish our drinks and play another game or two. Thanks, anyway, Olivia."

"Of course. Mrs. Clayborn, I hope you and your husband will seriously consider joining our club. Mother Berry has told us of your husband's very generous gift to the drama program at the school. That's particularly gratifying since my daughter-in-law is leading the department there."

"Thank you, Mrs. Grant. Shall we finish our tea, Bennie?"

Bennie and Laura watched as Olivia rejoined the ladies in her lunch group.

"Her daughter-in-law is leading the department." Bennie shook her head. "A department of one." She picked up her tennis racquet. "Let's go. I don't want to play any more with her watching."

Bennie led the way back to the ladies' locker room. Laura tossed her racket onto an ottoman, looked around the room, and plopped down in one of the chintz chairs. "It appears we have the place to ourselves."

"The golfers are probably just making the turn at the tenth tee. I'm going to shower. Are you?"

"Right now, I'm going to watch." Laura gave Bennie a lascivious grin and winked.

Bennie smiled and started stripping off her tennis outfit. First, she pulled her polo shirt over her head and unhooked her bra. She bent over and slowly and deliberately untied her tennis shoes and took off her socks. She heard Laura's gasp and the beginning of a whispered comment, "Bennie, you're..." Bennie put her finger to her lips. She stepped out of her short tennis skirt and panties and, without looking at Laura, turned and walked naked toward the showers. As she passed the vanity mirror, she saw Laura's reflection, motionless in the chair, her gaze following Bennie's retreating backside.

Bennie stepped into the small dressing area connected to one of the showers and pulled the plastic privacy curtain closed behind her. Two fluffy towels and a terry cloth robe lay neatly folded on a tiled bench. She picked up a new bar of lilac-scented soap and sniffed it. She turned the water as hot as she could stand, moved under the stream, and lathered her face and shoulders. She heard the scrape of the curtain being pulled back and felt someone stepping under the shower behind her.

Laura whispered in her ear. "If you're quiet, no one will know."

Bennie leaned into Laura and felt the imprint of her breasts and thighs. Her heart thudded against her ribs with both arousal and nervousness at the risk they were taking. Laura turned Bennie and kissed her hard, pressing her against the tile and taking the soap bar from her. She held Bennie's hands over her head against the wall while she worked the soap between their bodies, rubbing the lilac-scented bar over Bennie's breasts and belly and between her legs. Bennie closed her eyes and squeezed her lips shut, suppressing tell-tale sounds of her passion.

"Turn around." Laura massaged Bennie's buttocks with the soap, and then returned to stroking back and forth between her legs. Bennie arched her back rhythmically against the pressure, and she clutched Laura's hand as she climaxed. Her legs gave way, and she slid down the tile to sit on the floor, pulling Laura down with her.

"God."

The sound of water being turned on in the cubicle next door made them both jump. Bennie stood and turned off the water in their shower, handed Laura the robe, and pushed her outside the curtain. Bennie silently counted to ten, and ten again for good measure, dried off with one of the towels, and wrapped the other around herself.

The dressing area was beginning to fill with women coming from lunch or golfing. Laura was already half dressed in her street clothes. Bennie sat at the vanity and watched Laura in the mirror gathering her things and leaving. Bennie quickly changed and sat down again in front of the vanity mirror to towel dry her hair. The mirror reflected her flushed face and dilated pupils. She could still feel the pressure of Laura's hand against her body.

Bennie found Laura at the check-in desk by the front door, writing something while Ina looked on with her usual obsequious smile. Laura signed her name with a flourish and held the note for Bennie to read.

Dear Mrs. Grant,

Thank you so much for your hospitality. I thoroughly enjoyed my visit to your club. The tennis was a treat, and I especially enjoyed the lovely ladies' dressing area with its great shower facilities. I suspect you had a hand in the décor. Please tell your son I'll be giving my husband all the details.

Fondly, Laura Clayborn

Laura handed the note to Ina. "You'll make sure to give this to Mrs. Grant Senior, won't you?"

"Certainly. I'll take it to her personally right now."

In the car, Laura reached across the seat and took Bennie's hand. "Are you sure you can't spare the time to have dinner with me?"

"Laura, I promised myself I wouldn't see you again. I've got one more week of school, then a month left on my deal with Will. These last few weeks are dangerously important, and I don't seem to be able to control myself with you."

Laura lightly massaged Bennie's palm with her fingertips. "Don't worry about that. I can control both of us for a few weeks. Besides, sometimes what you deny yourself can be as erotic as what you act on."

Laura turned into the driveway in front of Bennie's residence hall, stopped the car, and turned off the motor. "Will you live here after the end of the term?"

"I've given Mother Berry notice that I won't be teaching next year. I'll start looking for a place for Livie and me right after the madness of graduation. I think Mother Berry will let me stay until I find something suitable. I'll help out by straightening up the library or doing something in the office."

Laura leaned across Bennie and peered out the car window at the residence hall's façade. "Wouldn't you rather be out of here as soon as possible? You are welcome to stay in my guesthouse for as long as you need. From what you've told me about Will, things may not go as smoothly as you hope. I've been thinking about getting a caretaker for the house anyway. This hotel project will keep me in Manhattan most weekends for the foreseeable future."

Bennie hesitated. "That's generous of you, but…"

"If you're worried about controlling things between us, I'll hardly be there. Go over sometime this week and look at the place. Here's the key." Laura took it off her keyring and handed it to Bennie. "And here's the code to the front gate." She wrote some numbers on a slip of paper from her purse. "I think you'd find my guesthouse a comfortable paradise after that little room of yours. If you're right about the Will business, it's only for a few weeks."

Chapter Seventeen

Graduation at Mary Bradford's was a hectic affair stretching over several days. It included Maypole dances by the freshmen and candlelight songfests with the entire student body. The week culminated with commencement and the seniors, dressed in identical long white gowns, marching to receive their diplomas.

Bennie waited until the week was over to approach Mother Berry about staying on for a while in her residence hall room. She was surprised when the headmistress turned her down with the reason that, since Miss Dodie would be taking over her classes and residence hall duties, the room needed to be available as soon as possible.

She wondered if Mother Berry was upset with her for quitting her post, or whether Olivia had some hand in making sure Bennie was uprooted. She guessed Laura was right about Mother Berry. Once Bennie was of no more use to the school, she was expendable.

The key to Laura's guesthouse and code to the gate were lying on her desk, next to Laura's business card. Laura's offer seemed sincere, and hadn't she said she'd be in New York most of the time? Bennie decided the guesthouse was a good solution. She tried calling Laura's Manhattan number but got no answer. She packed her things that afternoon and piled them into a taxi for the drive to Laura's weekend house.

The guesthouse sat on a knoll behind the main house and across a grassy courtyard, its back wall facing the woods beyond. It was a negative image of the main house. Instead of glass walls, the smaller guesthouse was a rectangular box of ground-to-roof red brick with no openings in the front façade except for a charcoal-colored front door. The door opened into a long corridor, illuminated by skylights. To the left, the corridor led to a large bedroom with an oval window covering almost the entire rear wall.

Back in the corridor, Bennie passed a bathroom and a small efficiency kitchen with stainless steel appliances matching those in the main house. At the other end of the corridor was a reading room, an oval window matching the one in the bedroom, and floor-to-ceiling bookshelves with plenty of empty space for Bennie to put her plays. Laura hadn't exaggerated. It was paradise compared to the residence hall.

She dialed Laura's New York number again but still got unanswered rings. Bennie hesitated to call the work number. Laura said she was insanely busy. Laura seemed insistent that she wanted Bennie to have the place, but Bennie hesitated to unpack before talking with her. She stacked her boxes of clothes and books in the reading room, walked into the village for a few breakfast essentials, ate an early supper at the Inn, and was back in the guesthouse asleep by nine o'clock.

Sometime in the middle of the night, Bennie heard a car door slam, but she wasn't sure if it was real or if she was dreaming. The next morning, she looked out and discovered Laura's car parked next to the house. She brewed a fresh pot of coffee and placed the coffeepot and two mugs on a tray she found on a shelf over the refrigerator. She debated taking time to dress but instead put a robe on over her pajamas. The early morning spring sunshine reflected off the back wall of the main house. Shading her eyes, Bennie could see Laura sitting on a stool at the counter in the kitchen, reading a newspaper.

Bennie balanced the tray in one hand and knocked on the glass. Laura looked up with a surprised smile. She gestured for Bennie to go around to the front door. As Bennie passed the car, she noticed two coats thrown haphazardly into the back seat.

Laura opened the door. "Come in. You're here. Did you stay last night? Have you decided to take me up on my offer?"

"I tried to call you, but things happened so fast."

"You brought us some coffee. How nice." Laura took the tray from Bennie and pulled out a stool for her at the counter.

A young woman came around the corner of the walnut cabinets separating the bed area from the rest of the house. She was barefoot and wore the same burgundy robe Laura had draped over Bennie's naked shoulders that first morning. The girl was tall and thin with dark hair and enormous brown eyes.

"Carolyn, come and meet Bennie." Laura rose from the stool and put an arm around Carolyn's waist.

Neither Bennie nor Carolyn spoke. Bennie was mute from surprise and Carolyn, it appeared to Bennie, from reticence.

"I've told Carolyn all about you, and now she gets to meet you in person." Laura smiled at Carolyn. "Bennie is going to be staying in the guesthouse for a time. This is perfect. I have to go back into the city for a few days of meetings with the hotel people. You two can keep each other company until I get back. Carolyn can cook dinner for you. She's a great cook. Aren't you, darling?"

The girl looked from Laura to Bennie. "Of course, if you want to have dinner together. Don't think we have to babysit each other though."

"Let's sit at the table so we can talk." Laura chattered away about the hotel job and how Carolyn was the best design assistant and essential to Laura's project. "She quit me for a little while, didn't you? But I've convinced her to come back, haven't I? She's going to start again in a week or so."

Carolyn nodded and sipped her coffee.

As soon as she could, Bennie made an excuse to leave. Back in the guesthouse, she threw herself on the bed and dug the heels of her hands into her eyes. Alice had been so right. She was crazy to get involved with Laura, who apparently expected to have her own little harem right in New Canaan. Laura acted as though having the two of them there was the most natural thing in the world. Bennie was definitely not interested. She yearned to talk to Alice, and made a snap decision. She wouldn't just talk to her. She would go to San Francisco after all.

She phoned Pan Am and reserved a seat from LaGuardia for the next day before calling the Mark Hopkins for a hotel room. She sent three telegrams. The first was to Alice, HOPE YOU STILL WANT ME. WILL CALL WHEN I LAND TOMORROW NIGHT. The second was to her father in Portland, IN SAN FRANCISCO AT MARK HOPKINS, THEN PORTLAND IF OK. LEAVING YOUR NUMBER AS A CONTACT FOR WILL. The last was to Will at his office, VISITING FATHER FOR A FEW DAYS. WILL CALL LIVIE EVERY DAY.

She stacked the boxes with her clothes and books in the bedroom closet and wrote a vaguely-worded note to Laura about an unexpected trip to the West Coast. She was relieved to hear a car door slam and the receding crunch of tires on the driveway.

Chapter Eighteen

The next morning, Bennie sat by the window in the waiting area of Gate One at LaGuardia Airport and watched her bag being loaded on Pan Am Flight 636 to San Francisco. Practically every seat in the waiting area was taken with businessmen reading their morning newspapers, women in smart traveling suits and hats, and one or two young couples who Bennie decided were on their honeymoons.

She tried reading a few pages from *Summer and Smoke* again, but it hadn't improved with time, and her mind kept wandering to the image of Carolyn coming around the corner of the room divider, barefoot and wearing the burgundy robe. There was no mistaking the situation. Laura and Carolyn had slept together. Did Bennie have any right to make a claim on Laura? What did it say about Laura that she could experience that kind of intimacy with more than one person at the same time?

Her thoughts were interrupted by the loudspeaker calling her flight. She took the doorway outside onto the tarmac and joined the line of other travelers climbing the plane's steps. Stewardesses in military-style uniforms helped them to their seats and took their coats. With loud backfires that made Bennie jump, the four engines started the sustained drone of propellers. Once they were airborne, she pulled the curtain over her window and fell into an exhausted sleep.

Nine and a half hours later, she hailed a cab in front of San Francisco Municipal Airport for the trip downtown to her hotel. As the cab turned off Market Street onto Powell, Bennie gasped. "It's straight up!"

The taxi driver looked at her in the rearview mirror. "First time in San Francisco?" Without waiting for an answer, he said, "That's Nob Hill. Not quite the steepest in the city, but close. There are seven hills, like Rome." He continued the impromptu guided tour, pointing out Union Square, the St. Francis Hotel, and at the top of the hill, before the taxi turned left onto California, the ornate gate marking the entrance to Chinatown. "Beyond there is North Beach, and beyond that, the Bay." He pulled into the brick forecourt of the Mark Hopkins Hotel and tipped his hat. "There you are, lady. A cab ride and a guided tour all in one."

Bennie paid the fare with a big tip and followed a bellman carrying her bag through the revolving front door with a stylized MH on the ornate crest above the entry. Two huge crystal chandeliers dominated the lobby area, crowded with smartly dressed men and women, sitting in small groups or walking to and from the elevators.

Bennie stepped up to the reception desk in front of a smiling clerk. His nametag read "Mr. Hodgins, Assistant Manager."

"You're busy, Mr. Hodgins. I expected the hotel to be quieter somehow."

"Yes, Madam. We are quite sought after at this time of year. We have a lovely quiet room for you on the fourteenth floor with a beautiful view. I'm sure you'll find it more than satisfactory."

As soon as she was settled in her room and unpacked, Bennie telephoned Livie. She was relieved when Haskins answered the phone and put her daughter on right away. She wasn't in any mood to deal with Olivia. Her daughter was full of news about her latest riding lesson and a new friend she had made at school who had a pony too. "Daddy says we might be able to ride together if Janice says it's okay."

"That's very exciting, darling." Bennie suddenly was on the verge of crying. She was so separated from her child, not just by three thousand miles, but more by the circumstances of the last few months and the prospect of what was to come. She cleared her throat and took a deep breath. "I'll go now, Livie. I love you. I'll call you tomorrow."

Bennie felt so desperate for all the waiting to be over that she almost didn't care how the custody fight came out. Maybe Livie would be better off with her father and Olivia. She sat on the edge of the bed with her head in her hands. She felt weak and afraid and selfish. She rose and went to stand at the window, looking out over the sweeping view from the Ferry Building to Golden Gate Park. She spoke to her reflection in the window glass. "Get a grip on yourself."

She was tired, not physically but mentally. She could use a distraction. She found a leather portfolio on the desk, filled with colorful pamphlets and maps describing the sights of the city. She pulled out one about Chinatown, located a few short blocks from the hotel. On the front was a picture of the gate to the district, a miniature version of the entrance to the Forbidden City with a green ceramic tile roof and parapets decorated with sea dragons and stylized dolphins. She decided a walk through Chinatown would be just the thing to settle her mind and her nerves before calling Alice.

Daylight was fading, and fog gathered at the level of the streetlights, shaped like decorative lanterns, lining Grant Street. Locals carrying net grocery bags jammed the sidewalk. Rainbow-colored neon signs in English and Chinese competed for the shoppers' attention, advertising chop suey, foreign movies, and noodle houses.

Bennie strolled along window-shopping, taking in the strange smells and unfamiliar cacophony of sounds. Each block had its own market with a loyal throng of customers crowded into narrow aisles between refrigerated cases of exotic seafood and stacked cardboard boxes of mysterious fruits and vegetables. She ventured inside one of the markets and passed by a jumbled stack of strange creatures she thought must be dried sea cucumbers. Customers were lined up in front of a lighted display case with fish and meats. Bennie jumped in surprise as she passed a glass tank filled with toads, their dead eyes wide open and staring.

Back on the street, she cringed at the sight of denuded smoked ducks hanging by their necks in the front window of a poultry store. She marveled at baskets of unfamiliar and strong-smelling dried roots, nuts, and leaves outside an herbalist.

She turned into the door of the shop. A tiny brass bell tinkled, announcing her presence. Once her eyes adjusted to the dim interior, she could see that every wall was lined to the ceiling with small drawers, labeled with Chinese characters. An ancient-looking wooden ladder with wheels on the bottom attached to a track in the ceiling provided access to the hundreds of drawers.

The herbalist, dressed in a traditional black silk tunic, stood at attention behind the counter. Bennie was surprised to see he wore dark-lensed glasses in the gloomy shop. He bowed slightly and spoke, looking just past her.

"May I help you, Madam?"

"I was wondering if you have anything to improve one's courage."

At the sound of her voice, the herbalist adjusted his gaze slightly to address her directly. He was blind. "Ah, are you seeking moral courage or physical courage?"

"I think it's both—the moral courage to know what's right, and the physical courage to carry through with it."

"A wise answer." The man nodded as he pulled a small empty paper bag from under the counter. He stood facing the wall of drawers behind him. "As you no doubt can observe, finding the proper drawer in my mind's eye takes me a moment. Yes, that's what we're looking for." He rolled the ladder a few feet to the left and climbed to near the top. He filled the bag, half from one drawer and half from a drawer beside it. After climbing nimbly back down the ladder, he took a thick red grease pencil, drew several Chinese characters on the bag, and held it across the counter toward Bennie.

"What does it say?"

"It says courage is knowing what not to fear."

Outside, the fog had thickened and formed halos around the neon signs, softening their garish colors. The cloud of fog made Bennie feel as though she was wrapped in damp cotton and isolated from the noise of the street and the crowds of people.

She opened the paper bag and sniffed the contents. It smelled of a mixture of cloves, mint, and damp soil. She made a slight face. Bennie decided she would settle for a different kind of courage by going back to her room, ordering a Manhattan, and then thinking about calling Alice.

Alice picked up on the first ring, and her enthusiasm left Bennie breathless. Hearing Alice's voice reminded Bennie how much she had missed her friend. Just talking to her on the phone was a boost. "I've missed you so much, my friend."

"I'm so anxious to see you. If you want to rest tonight, we can start in the morning with a visit to Golden Gate Park, then lunch at the Buena Vista Café, very much an insider's place down by the Bay".

"Wait, Alice. Take a breath."

"I'm sorry," Alice said. "I know part of the purpose of this trip is rest and relaxation for you. Reel me back in when I get higher than a kite about your being here. Anyway, back to tomorrow's itinerary. I've hired a car and driver for the whole day, so we can mosey around the park and its museums as long as we like. I think you'll especially enjoy the de Young Museum."

"It sounds wonderfully restful and relaxing. Can we talk first thing in the morning? I'm halfway into a Manhattan and starting to feel the time change."

Chapter Nineteen

The next morning, a knock on Bennie's door announced room service breakfast. The waiter quietly and efficiently set up a table with a white linen cloth, a crystal glass for orange juice, and fine China with the signature MH logo. He had no sooner let himself out of the room when the phone rang.

"I hope I'm not calling too early. I can pick you up in an hour. Bev has planned a little dinner party for this evening. She wants you to see her house, which is quite a showplace, and introduce you to a few of our friends. Nothing fancy." Alice spoke so fast she was breathless.

"I'm overwhelmed. What did you say about reeling you back in like a kite?" Bennie smiled and shook her head.

"Too much? I know, I know. I promise to come back down to earth after today. We can skip the Buena Vista Café if you like."

"We'll see. I'll expect you at ten or so?"

"Great."

Bennie poured another cup of coffee and called her father. He sounded glad to hear from her, but his voice held a tinge of concern.

"What's this about, Bennie? It seems like a strange, spur-of-the-moment trip."

"Alice lives here in San Francisco now, and she invited me to visit. I wasn't sure I could get away, but as things developed, I was able to after all. I want to see you, Father. It's been a long time, and a few things are happening that I could use your advice about."

"What things? Is Livie all right? Is this something between you and Will?"

"Livie is thriving. She got a new pony for Christmas, and she's learning to jump." Bennie paused. "Can we talk about the rest when I see you? It's complicated. I'll call you in a few days when my travel plans are firm." Bennie rushed to eat her breakfast and dress in time to meet Alice in the lobby.

***

Alice was the perfect enthusiastic tour guide around the large urban green space of Golden Gate Park.

"It's bigger than Central Park." Alice was already proud of her newly-adopted city. "It's a thousand acres to Central Park's eight hundred. There were times when the park was first built that half the city's population would crowd in on a Sunday afternoon."

By the time they toured the park's two art museums, the Japanese Garden, and North and South windmills, it was three in the afternoon. Bennie stopped at a bench. She sat down and rubbed her calves. "Please tell me your legs are as tired as mine."

Alice checked her watch. "It's the perfect time to go to the Buena Vista for a drink."

In the tiny café overlooking the Bay, they found two seats together at a big table in the back of the crowded room.

"It's the custom here to share tables wherever you can find empty seats." Alice winked at Bennie and inclined her head toward a pretty blond woman across the table. "You never know who you'll meet."

They ordered the Irish Coffee that the Buena Vista claimed to have invented and watched the performance of the bartender lining up ten glasses in a row and pouring the right amount of whiskey in a steady stream across them without spilling a drop.

They sipped their cocktails and enjoyed the view of the Bay. Bennie reached across the table and squeezed Alice's hand. "Today has been wonderfully entertaining. I've missed you so much. Can we walk down by the water for a while? I've got something to talk over with you, and maybe the fresh salt air will clear my head."

"Okay. I'll let the driver go, and we can take the cable car to your hotel from here. That's another San Francisco must-do experience."

After Alice paid the bill, they followed the sidewalk down the steep hill to the Bay and turned toward North Beach. The day was clear, and the water of the Bay was calm. Alcatraz Island appeared close enough that an inmate could swim to freedom. They walked along in companionable silence.

"This is hard for me to admit, Alice, because I've been very foolish, against your sage advice." Bennie waited for a response, but Alice merely shook her head.

Bennie took Alice's arm. "You're going to make me tell it all, aren't you? I may be selfish confiding in you, given the feelings you've had for me, but you're the only one I can talk to." She paused and took a deep breath. "I've gotten involved with Laura Clayborn. I know you suspected I might. What's worse, now I've found out I mean nothing to her. I've put my relationship with my child in jeopardy for nothing."

Alice's kept silent as they continued to walk.

Bennie turned Alice so they made eye contact. "Say something. Do you want to hear details? Ask me any questions, and I'll answer honestly."

"No, no." Alice held her hands up, as if to shield herself from Bennie's revelations. "Details about your affair with someone else are the last things I want to hear."

Bennie felt a heavy weight of guilt on her heart. Alice didn't deserve to be subjected to this, but Bennie had no one else.

Alice sighed and looked across the Bay. "I am willing to be your friend, though, if I can. What makes you say you mean nothing to her?"

"Well, she's married, happily as far as I know, so not completely available. Now I find out she's involved with another woman at the same time as me. It's that girl she brought to the dinner party where you met Laura, her design assistant."

"How do you know she's involved with her?"

"Carolyn, the girl, spent the night with Laura at her house in New Canaan."

"Did Laura break her word about that or lie to you about it?"

"No. She seemed to think it was fine that we were both there."

"Did you talk to her about it?"

Bennie looked down at the sidewalk. "No. I left her a note and got a plane out without talking to her at all."

The breeze off the Bay had grown stiffer, and both women pulled their coats tighter around their bodies.

"Bennie, how old would you say Laura is—ten years older than us or so?"

"Thereabouts."

"She came up before the war. Things are difficult enough for us now, but they were even worse then. She has set up a double life—a public one, married to a man, and a hidden one with women. She's used to episodic relationships. It's normal for her."

"I don't think I could be happy living that way."

Alice nodded. "I don't have to tell you I've done my share of that, but I know you couldn't be happy with a double life. If you could, you and I might still be together." Alice's voice turned sharp. "I can't tell if you're more concerned about Laura's being married or her being involved with both you and Carolyn at the same time. Which is it?"

Bennie thought hard before answering. "More her involvement with the girl. She says her marriage is one of convenience."

"Would you want her to leave him for you? Would she do that?"

"I don't know."

"I don't think it's fair for you to judge Laura by your standards, especially since you're not exactly clear about your own direction. If you care about her, shouldn't you at least give her a chance to tell you what she's thinking?"

"I was embarrassed and afraid I had assumed too much."

They walked a little farther in the gathering twilight.

"It seems all I do anymore is lecture you, and that's not my style. It's getting late. Lecture done. Let's go back and catch the cable car."

Across from the Buena Vista, they watched a cable car pull onto the giant turntable which reversed the car's direction for the return trip to Market Street. Bennie was fascinated to see the ticketholders, who had been waiting in the long line, pitch in to help turn the heavy car. Instead of joining the line at the turnaround, Bennie and Alice walked up the hill and jumped on as the car slowed for a red light.

"Another insider trick." Alice laughed as they took seats on a bench facing the street.

"It's marvelous what you can see from out here." Bennie leaned over to look back down the steep hill. She applauded when the grip man played his signature cadence on the cable car's bell. She glanced at Alice. "I've missed doing things like this since you left. You mean so much to me."

"I know."

Alice checked her watch when they jumped off the car at the corner of Powell and California. "Your hotel is just there, in the middle of the block. I'll catch a taxi from here. There will be plenty of time for you to relax before dinner. We'll start about eight, and remember, very informal. There will only be ten of us or so."

Back in her hotel room, Bennie ran a tub of water and added bath salts. Her leg and hip muscles ached from the unaccustomed walking in the hilly city. She sighed in contentment as she sank into the tub with a magazine she found on her bedside table. The magazine, *Inside the City by the Bay*, featured a cover article about Bev's house.

The house was built over a hundred years earlier by a former mayor of San Francisco. When Bev bought it, the old place had fallen into disrepair. The article showed remarkable before and after pictures. Bennie was excited to see the house and meet Alice's new friends.

Chapter Twenty

The afternoon's clear weather held into the evening. There was no sign of the fog Bennie walked through in Chinatown the night before. As her taxi headed west toward Pacific Heights, she remembered the first and only time she met Bev, twelve years earlier, when Bev was Alice's roommate in college. Bennie pictured a serious, focused, attractive young woman who already knew she wanted to be an architect. Her personality was the polar opposite of Alice's.

The taxi dropped her in front of the house. Bennie stood at the curb admiring the mansion and the Golden Gate Bridge, outlined with hundreds of lights, in the distance. The Queen Anne Victorian house stood on the corner of two streets at the apex of a hill. The streets and sidewalks fell precipitously away, giving the impression that the house was a gemstone set in a fancy ring.

The house was painted with two shades of green and burnt sienna trim. *These must be the original colors of the house.* Bev would have done the research. The house had three gables and several bay windows. It was covered in fish scale shingles.

Bennie climbed the wide front steps. The front door was slightly ajar and she recognized Alice's laughter in response to a male voice. She hesitated, unsure whether to ring the bell, call out, or push the door open. She decided on ringing the bell, and in a moment Bev appeared at the door. "Come in, Bennie. Alice is being held in thrall by Peter. Almost everyone else is here already."

Bev was casually dressed in grey flannel slacks and a green silk blouse, tucked in to emphasize her slim waist and hips and accented with an expensive-looking leather belt. Her dark hair, a stark contrast to her amazing green eyes, was cut shoulder-length.

Bennie turned in a full circle in the foyer. She thought of Laura and how impressed she would be with the house. "Let me stand here for a moment and admire this space. The millwork on the paneling and stairs is remarkable."

"You have a good eye. You couldn't buy these rare woods today, much less find the workmen to craft them. Bringing the house back to her glory was the most daunting and, at the same time, most satisfying thing

I've done. Truth be told, I suspect it's what brought me to the attention of the ballet company board of directors. Alice told you about my project, right?"

"She certainly did. Congratulations."

"And you are interested in the theater. You'll be right in tune with at least half of our guests." Bev took Bennie's arm and steered her into the drawing room.

Instead of the stiff, formal furniture fashionable in the late 1800s, Bev had decorated the room with comfortable upholstered chairs and sofas in light-colored fabrics. Spotlights illuminated an impressive collection of Northern California Impressionist paintings of seascapes, poppy and lupine fields, and eucalyptus trees. Cut flowers were on every table, their colors complementing the upholstery and muted tones in the paintings. On the west wall facing them was the centerpiece of the room, a massive wine-colored marble fireplace.

When the two women entered the room, conversation stopped, and Alice and four guests turned toward them in unison. The scene reminded Bennie of a tableau of attractive people in a tasteful room.

Bev broke the spell. "Everyone, this is Bennie Grant."

Alice rushed forward and embraced Bennie. "Come in and meet everyone. Bennie, this is Tony and over there, his wife, Avery. I'll use first names."

The couple smiled and nodded. "This man, who's been regaling us with inside opera gossip, is Peter, and over next to Avery is Michael. We're all having champagne. Bev, will get you a glass?"

Alice turned back to Peter. "Now, Peter, you must get to know Bennie. She's very interested in stage directing. Peter's the chorus director for our opera company, but he's so much more, really. He practically runs the whole thing. The general director is in such ill health, but he'll die with a baton in his hand, won't he, Peter?"

Bennie and Peter shook hands, and she excused herself to help Bev with the champagne. "This room is beautiful. I've never seen such a stunning collection of Impressionist paintings."

"The paintings are a particularly California thing. The artists are just now being widely discovered. I've been lucky to happen on some real finds." Bev looked around the room. "I am proud of the place. I try to stop short of being a bore about it."

"You've every right to be proud."

The sound of a doorbell interrupted them, and Bev headed to answer it, handing Michael the champagne bottle as she passed him. "That's the prima ballerina now. They're the last. Michael, fill everyone's glasses."

Michael smiled shyly at Bennie and shifted the champagne bottle to shake her hand.

"I'm Michael. I'm here with Peter." He was young and handsome in a typical California way—tall with an athletic build, and light hair which he wore rather long. "Did she say a prima ballerina is at the door?"

"That's what she said."

Bev entered the room with a woman dressed in black slacks and a black turtleneck sweater. She wore a bright fuchsia silk scarf around her neck. She was tall and slender, with no sign of womanly curves. Her light-colored hair was straight and parted in the middle. Her heavy-lidded blue eyes sparkled as she surveyed the room with a confident smile. Her gaze settled on Bennie for a moment too long for casual interest.

"Everyone, this is Dame Renata Glenn, San Francisco Ballet's guest ballet mistress for this season."

Renata made a small bow. "Oh, Bev, not so formal. Titles are for performance program notes, not for everyday life. Just Renata, please." Her accent was distinctly British. She strode into the room and introduced herself to each guest with a handshake. Her hands were unusually large, her gaze disturbingly direct. She clearly knew Peter well. Bennie watched as she embraced him and kissed him on both cheeks.

When she was introduced to Bennie, Renata leaned in. "Bennie. What is Bennie short for?"

"Just Bennie. It's not short for anything."

"Charming."

The doorbell sounded again.

Renata looked toward the door. "Yuri was trying to settle with the taxi driver. He hasn't quite figured out your money yet."

When Bev escorted the young man into the room, Renata introduced him as a guest dancer who was performing with the San Franciscan company. He could have been Renata's twin, except he was much younger. He wore a similar black turtleneck and slacks, minus the fuchsia scarf, outlining a similar slim physique. Both of them moved with the distinctive glide that Bennie had noticed in other dancers. They never seemed to simply walk like other mortals but appeared to float upright in perfect balance.

At dinner, Bennie sat between Tony and Avery. The couple were engaging and interesting, with fascinating stories about their family's history as pioneers in the wine industry in Napa Valley. Tony recently split with his brothers in a dispute over which varieties of grapes to grow and started his own new label.

Renata sat directly across the table from Bennie. Throughout dinner she was absorbed in lively conversation with Peter, from time-to-time glancing at Bennie.

Over dessert, Renata leaned toward Bennie. "Alice tells me you're a stage director."

"She overstates it. I've directed in a community theater, and I taught drama at a girls' school, but I'm between things now."

"But you aspire to direct on Broadway?"

"Yes, I do." For the first time since Bennie left school and married, she allowed herself to fully own her ambition by saying it aloud, without qualifiers. The statement made her smile.

After dinner, the guests regrouped in the living room. Bev served coffee, along with a special brandy Tony had brought. Renata claimed the chair next to Bennie. "I'm making a change professionally myself, not dancing much anymore. I plan to do more choreographing, which has a lot in common with stage directing. Dancing takes a toll on one." She stretched her long legs in front of her and pointed to her toes. "If you could see what years of toe shoes have done to my poor feet." She laughed. "That isn't a very attractive image to present to such a beautiful woman as you, is it?"

Bennie smiled. "It's evidence of your dedication to your art, I suppose. I have to admit to a deep ignorance about your world. Is changing from performing to choreography difficult?"

"I've made a first step by being ballet mistress here in San Francisco. I hope that will lead to choreography. But to answer your question directly—yes, it's difficult for a woman choreographer to know any success in the ballet world. I suspect things are similar for women trying to be successful stage directors. I have some contacts in New York that could be helpful to you."

"That's kind of you."

Alice clapped her hands, interrupting her guests' conversations. "Let's play Three Questions. It's a way we can get to know each other better. We go around the room, and each person answers three questions. Where were you born? How many siblings do you have? And what was your greatest challenge growing up? After you've answered the three questions, you choose the next person to answer the questions."

There was some good-natured grumbling from a few guests.

Bev settled into a chair. "No sense resisting. She won't relent. I've learned to relax and enjoy it, and I usually wind up having fun. Consider it singing for your supper. I'll even go first. I was born in University Park, Pennsylvania."

Tony interrupted. "Penn State."

"That's right. My father was an assistant football coach there. I had four older brothers, and I suppose that led to my biggest challenge growing up. I was another member of my father's burgeoning home-grown football team until puberty struck. Overnight, or anyway that's the way it seemed to me, he lost interest in me. That was the challenge, but I changed my focus from football to a fascination with architecture. And here I am today."

"Brava!" Peter applauded.

"Thank you, Peter, and for that you go next."

"What are the questions again?"

Alice ticked them off on her fingers. "Where were you born? How many siblings do you have? What was your biggest challenge growing up?"

"Vienna, one younger brother, and the collapse of the Hapsburg monarchy."

The group laughed.

"Explain the Hapsburg part for those of us who might not be up on European history."

"My father was Home Secretary in Austria during the First War. Before the war, we led a privileged life, private schools, servants, the works. During the war, things were difficult. I don't need to go into all that. After the war, Austria became a republic with an entirely different power structure. Overnight, my family went from privileged class to middle class. Not such a horrible thing from most Americans' point of view, but quite traumatic for my family, especially my mother. Living with the depth of her unhappiness was hard. She focused her attention on me becoming a virtuoso pianist. I tried, heaven knows, but I'm just not that talented."

Renata patted Peter's arm. "You're a virtuoso opera director though."

"Thank you for the compliment, my dear, and would you like to go next?"

"I will." Renata paused.

Bennie watched Renata take the stage and wait until she had everyone's complete attention.

"I was born in London, an only child. My challenge came very young during my first year of school. I was underperforming in class, and my teacher complained to my mother that I was fidgety and lacked focus. My mother took me to a medical doctor. After hearing my mother's worries and concerns, he told me he needed to see my mother in private. Before they left the room, he turned on the radio. When he and Mother peeked back in on me, I was dancing madly around the room. 'She's a dancer,' the doctor told my mother. 'Stop worrying and enroll her right away in dance school.' And she did."

Renata's story drew applause from around the room. She stood and acknowledged the applause with a deep and graceful bow. She walked around the circle of guests, tapping her index finger to her lips. "Now. Whom to choose? Whom to choose?" She stopped before Bennie. "You've been quiet and mysterious all evening. You're next."

Bennie shook her head. "Hardly mysterious." When she saw all the attention turn in her direction, she went on. "In fact, I've been dreading answering the questions because I can't match any of your stories of challenges growing up. I simply didn't experience any. I was born an only child in Portland, Oregon, but raised in Connecticut by a doting grandmother who made sure my life was perfect."

"What about your parents? Where were they?" Michael asked.

"My father lived in Portland—still does—but he often traveled East for business. I saw him then, and whenever I did, it was special. My mother died when I was very young, before my memory. That's when I went to live in Connecticut."

"So your whole life has been perfect?" Renata sounded skeptical.

"Growing up, yes, it was."

Alice jumped in. "I'll go next, if I may, Bennie." She told her story and then called on Tony.

The remaining guests were chosen one after the other and each told their stories. Alice declared the game over, and Bev circulated among the guests offering a last glass of brandy. Most of them declined and began saying their goodbyes and finding their coats.

Bennie thanked Bev for dinner and hugged Alice. Renata moved to help Bennie with her coat. "If you're interested, you may want to come to rehearsal tomorrow. We're preparing for a two-week run of Balanchine's *Apollo.* The company rehearses and performs in the War Memorial Opera House, until the very talented Bev completes our new ballet hall."

Renata walked Bennie to a waiting cab and opened the door. "Come by rehearsal. I think you'll enjoy it."

"I just might."

Chapter Twenty-One

Bennie stood in front of the imposing Beaux-Arts style opera house and wondered if Bev's new ballet hall would be this formal or more modern. She went through the front doors between massive Doric columns and paused in the entrance hall to admire the high-gilded, barrel-vaulted ceiling. The auditorium doors were open, and she heard a piano playing as Renata's voice counted time.

Bennie took a seat halfway back in the empty auditorium. Renata was putting the corps de ballet through synchronized movements. She wore a blue smock over her black tights and carried a long wooden rod that she used to beat time and to correct the dancers' lines. "Higher legs, everyone, watch the angles."

She clapped her hands to stop the piano and walked to the edge of the stage to consult with two men sitting in the front row. One of them must be the choreographer. As though she had been watching for her, Renata noticed Bennie, shielded her eyes from the glare of the stage lighting, and waved. As Renata returned to the rehearsal, a young man ran up the side aisle to where Bennie sat.

"Dame Renata asks if you'd like to watch from the wing."

Bennie nodded and followed him to a side door leading up some stairs to the backstage area. She watched as Renata counted and corrected the corps members until they moved exactly the same, forming a perfect backdrop for the principal dancers. To Bennie's eye, one dancer stood out. All the dancers were graceful and appeared technically proficient, but one seemed to dance without thinking, her movements less rigid. Renata corrected her lines and angles more often to conform to the rest of the corps.

When it was finally time to quit for the day, Renata came toward her, wiping her face with a towel and smiling. "Bennie, I'm so glad you came after all. You hadn't said you would for sure. Let's go down to my little cubbyhole and have some tea."

Renata's room was tiny, furnished with a shabby upholstered sofa, chairs, and a small writing desk.

"Excuse my ugly digs. These old theaters never have enough space for everyone. I'm lucky to have any place private, I suppose. The better dressing rooms are reserved for the principal dancers."

"Do you miss performing?"

Renata plugged in an electric kettle to make their tea before answering. "Sometimes. I miss the nineteen curtain calls I used to get. In my day, I had choreographers lined up, begging me to dance for them, even writing ballets especially for me. But a dancer's repertoire shrinks as her number of years expands. I promised myself I'd quit dancing at thirty, then at thirty-five, and now I'm forty-two. Choreographers hunger for young, brilliant dancers who can make their works successful, I suppose as people in your field crave great actors."

"Honestly, it's overstating to call the theater my field."

The teakettle sounded a piercing whistle. Renata made their tea and sank with a sigh into the deep overstuffed chair across from Bennie on the sofa. She looked at Bennie with her direct gaze. "I didn't want to ask at dinner last night. I was concerned you might think I was prying. But if you have a passion for directing on the stage, why have you not pursued it? Do you question your talent?"

Bennie answered more sharply than she meant to. "I have a child to be concerned about."

"Excuse me for a moment." Renata left the room and returned with the young dancer Bennie had noticed during the corps de ballet rehearsal. "Bennie, this is my daughter, Giselle. Giselle, Mrs. Grant."

Giselle shook hands with Bennie and declined the cup of tea her mother offered. "I'm going out with Yuri and some others. Don't wait up for me." She threw the comment over her shoulder from the doorway as she left.

"Not too late. You need your sleep for rehearsal tomorrow." Renata was speaking to the closed door.

"She's lovely. I noticed her dancing in the corps rehearsal."

"She and I are struggling right now. Last season she was thrilled to be chosen for the corps, but this season, she's resisting the regimentation. She's anxious to dance a featured role. Yuri and some of the young choreographers don't help matters by filling her head with flattery. She will be very good, and perhaps great, but not yet."

Renata sat beside Bennie on the sofa and took her hand. "I had a purpose in introducing you to Giselle. You can tell me to mind my own business. There's nothing worse, or a bigger waste of time in my mind, than having to listen to the self-righteous, egocentric palaver of one who thinks she has all the answers. Just let me say that once I stood at the same crossroads where you stand—my passion or my child, I had to choose whether I would throw off 'the husk of convention' as someone called it."

Bennie remembered Laura saying Bennie's favorite word was convention.

Renata looked at the door where Giselle had stood. "I chose my passion. Giselle lived with my mother until she was fifteen when she began traveling with me, studying in whatever ballet school we were near at the time. There are many complicated facets to our relationship, but mother and daughter has rarely been one of them, as you could tell by that little exchange just now."

"With hindsight, would you make a different choice?"

"No, but I'm not suggesting my decision would be the right decision for you. You have to think first of your own completeness and whether you'll regret whatever decision you make. Regret is like a wasting disease. It can make you no good for yourself or your child."

Their tea had gotten cold, and Renata rose to put the kettle on again. "As I mentioned last night, I have a contact in New York, a woman who is the director of the American Repertory Theater. Let me know if you want an introduction. You would have to start at the bottom, of course."

"Of course. Just like Giselle in the corps de ballet."

Chapter Twenty-Two

The days and nights of the next week were busy. Every morning Bennie woke early enough to call Connecticut before Livie was off to school. After breakfast she met Alice for shopping in the exclusive stores around Union Square, lunch at one of the city's venerable restaurants, or drives north across the Golden Gate Bridge into forests of redwoods or through the vineyards of Napa Valley. Most evenings she joined Bev and Alice for dinner, often them and their friends, and always involving too many cocktails and too much wine.

After such an evening, Bev and Bennie sat with their brandy on Bev's balcony. Alice and Peter were behind them in the living room, playing gin rummy. Through the open doors, they could hear the sounds of a hard-fought, competitive game. Peter appeared to be getting the better of Alice.

Alice protested loudly. "You said you hardly know how to play this game."

Peter laughed. "I'm getting lucky cards. That's all."

"Deal," Alice grumbled.

Bennie glanced at Bev, who appeared completely content as she stared toward the Bay over the rooftops of Pacific Heights. "Alice sent me a picture when she first came out here, and I'm sure she was standing on this very spot. She looked so excited to be here in that photo, and seeing her now, I can tell you make her happy."

"I appreciate you saying that, Bennie." Bev sipped her brandy. "You might have guessed I was apprehensive about your coming out for a visit. I tried not to show my insecurity to Alice. I've always known Alice was in love with you. She's a transparent person, which might explain why Peter is beating her at gin rummy."

The two women listened for a while to Peter and Alice's banter. Bev's cigarette lighter flared in the dark.

"Alice told me about your affair after you broke it off."

"I hope you know it's ancient history. I wish you and Alice all the happiness in the world."

Bev turned to look directly at Bennie for the first time. "I know you do. You see, your coming to San Francisco was the best thing that could have happened for Alice and me. Seeing you and Alice together, I think I understand you a little better. It will certainly help me give up my insecurities about Alice's feelings for you. I hope Alice and I can build a life together, and there's nothing that will kill a relationship faster than a lover who constantly needs reassurance of the other's commitment. Don't you agree?"

"Yes. That and infidelity." Again, the picture of Carolyn coming from Laura's bed flashed in Bennie's mind. She swirled the brandy in her glass. "I'm glad Alice has assured you it's over between us, and the two of you can move on."

"I don't mean to give you the wrong impression. She hasn't conveyed it in so many words, but as I said, Alice is a transparent person, and I can tell the spell is broken."

Bennie gasped involuntarily. "The spell? You make me out to be a witch. Is that what you call understanding me better?"

"You're not so much a witch as you are a sorceress, I suppose."

Bennie felt the color rise in her face and she was glad for the darkness on the balcony.

"Look, Bennie, far be it from me to psychoanalyze anyone, though I'll admit to having lots of experience on the receiving end of analysis. I know all of this must be difficult for you." Bev held up her hands. "Let me quit before I get completely out of line. I'm not exactly objective where Alice is concerned."

"How do you mean it must be difficult for me? What has Alice told you?"

"Alice is relatively tight-lipped about you. I'm just saying, you are a married woman with a child and all the responsibilities that go along with those roles, and yet you find yourself magnetizing women. Alice did say you may be involved with someone in New Canaan. Who knows what others?"

A memory of Janice Traynor taking her elbow on the street crossed Bennie's mind. Was she one of the women Bev was talking about?

Bev went on matter-of-factly, as though confident none of this was news to Bennie. "When it doesn't last, you have to deal with their disappointment after you draw them into a relationship and then can't sustain it."

Bennie rose from her chair and stood at the balcony railing, her hands balled into fists. "I don't feel comfortable talking with you about

Alice, as though she weren't sitting in the next room. I'll just say that my friendship with Alice is the most important thing in the world to me, next to my child, and I hope it's survived her disappointment that we couldn't go on any longer. I think it has."

Bennie turned to face Bev. She could barely make out her features in the darkness. "And I won't accept your characterization of me as some predator who goes around deliberately luring women into pointless affairs. Alice has loved me since we were children."

The light of Bev's cigarette glowed in the gloom. "This conversation has taken a wrong turn. I don't mean to characterize you at all. I simply mean to point out the irony that your coming to San Francisco, while it could have made me terribly jealous, has been a good thing for Alice and me...it was self-centered of me to take things in this other direction. Look, Bennie, I know you're not a bad person, just a little unconscious of how extraordinarily beautiful you are and of your impact on other people." Bev rose from her chair. "Let's go in and rescue Alice. She pretends losing at card games doesn't bother her, but you and I know better."

Bennie turned to looked out over the Bay. "You go ahead. Give me a minute." She needed to get her emotions under control before going in. She knew Alice could certainly read her upset over the conversation, and she was unwilling to get into this discussion with her.

Bev hesitated at the open door. "Bennie, really, I'm sorry. Honestly, I'm done being a bad hostess. I will make this offer though. You may think me an unlikely confidante but, sadly, I can draw upon lots of experience with the difficulties of relationships like ours. Call on me if you need to."

As soon as there was a break in the card game, Bennie asked Bev to call her a taxi. She felt anxious to be away from Bev and Alice and back to her hotel room. During the ride across the misty, roller-coaster streets of the city, she decided she'd had enough of San Francisco. The time had come to visit her father in Portland.

Back at the Mark Hopkins, she crossed the brightly lit, deserted hotel lobby on her way to the elevator. One lone clerk stood behind the ornately carved front desk facing the elevators, busy with paperwork. He looked up and nodded. "Good evening, Mrs. Grant."

"Good evening. Any messages for me?"

Bennie didn't expect any. Her father was the only one who knew where to reach her. She left Laura a vaguely-worded note. Laura was resourceful enough to track her down, but Bennie didn't expect she would.

"No, Ma'am."

Her room was freshly cleaned and smelled of lemons. Filmy curtains fluttered in the breeze from an open window. Across the canyon of urban San Francisco, she heard the echo of a cable car bell and smiled to herself remembering her ride with Alice. The turned-down bed invited her, but she decided to call the airline about a plane to Portland. The front desk rang the number, but she got a busy signal. *What crowd of people could be calling the airlines at this hour?* She hung up and drummed her fingers on the desk blotter.

She changed into pajamas and a robe. She was about to pick up the receiver and ask the front desk clerk to try again when there was a knock on her door. "Who is it?" she called sharply, her impatience with the airline carrying over.

"Bennie?"

"Laura?"

She rushed to the door and threw it open. At first Bennie had the ridiculous thought she must have conjured up the woman standing outside her door.

"Can I come in?"

"Yes, yes. What are you doing here? How did you find me?"

Laura looked around the room. She took off her gloves and hat and tossed them, along with her alligator purse, on the bed. "Your note said you were coming to the West Coast. I thought you'd see your father, so I got Mother Berry to give me his number. It was in your employment records. After some convincing, your father told me where to find you."

They stood facing each other, wordless, Bennie with her fists jammed into her robe pockets and Laura looking composed in her smart traveling suit.

Laura broke the silence. "May I?" she asked as she gestured toward the upholstered side chair flanking a coffee table.

Bennie nodded and sat down on the edge of the sofa.

Laura stood to retrieve her purse from the bed, took out a cigarette, lit it, and sat again. "All right, do you want to tell me what this is all about?"

Bennie tried to order her thoughts.

Laura stabbed out the cigarette in an ashtray. "Bennie, I've traveled all the way across the country for you. The least you can do is meet me halfway on talking this through. I'll say it. It's about Carolyn, isn't it? If you want me to go into all the details of that long story, at the risk of being indiscreet, I'll do so. Carolyn came to work for me after her graduation, one of several design assistants I had at the time. She had lots of potential and she reminded me of myself at that age—talented but inexperienced. I gave her extra attention, mentoring her, and we spent time together outside of work, at her initiation, but I'll own that I should have set some boundaries. She started showing up at our apartment and then staying overnight. Things got out of hand. Charles, who almost never interferes with my life, saw the problem much clearer than I did and put his foot down. By then, Carolyn's work was suffering, and the other staff were becoming resentful of her special treatment. So I broke it off, I think as gently as possible."

Bennie tried to imagine how such a breakup could have been done gently. She could imagine how devastated the young girl would have been.

Laura went on. "She went off the deep end. She quit work…just walked out and disappeared. I didn't want to lose her. I care about her, but I want us to keep things on a professional basis. I hired a private investigator to find her and then took her to the house in New Canaan that night because it's peaceful, and I thought it would be a good setting to talk things out. That's where you came in. I didn't know you had decided to take me up on my offer of the guesthouse."

"I tried calling you." Bennie leaned forward. "Did you sleep with her?"

"That's the question you want to ask? Sleep, yes, but that's all. I reasoned with her and consoled her, and she agreed to come back to work with me, and then we went to sleep. And here's a question for you." Laura's words were clipped and her voice cold. "Why didn't you ask me this in New Canaan instead of running away?"

Bennie rose from the sofa and stared out the window at the streetlights lining Powell Street, descending Nob Hill to the Mission District. Each light threw off a halo reflected by the misty air. "It was so awkward, and I was embarrassed. I was afraid of hearing what I assumed you would say. Running away seems easier." Bennie glanced at the herbalist's small paper bag with red Chinese characters sitting on the desk, where she had left it the first day. *Courage is knowing what not to fear.* "And now you're angry with me for being such a coward."

Laura moved over to the sofa and patted the space next to her. Bennie sat down and Laura put her arm around her shoulders and held her close. "I was angry all week since you left and during the nine hours flying across the country, but the anger will burn itself out. Seeing you helps. I'm here now. Let's take the opportunity just to be together. I know you're looking at some hard times ahead with your divorce. Maybe I can help you forget that until you have to face things back home."

Bennie moved closer under Laura's arm and breathed deeply for the first time since Laura stepped into the room. "I'm planning to leave San Francisco and go to Portland to visit my father. I feel I've overstayed my welcome here."

Laura held her close and kissed the top of her head. "How have you overstayed your welcome? Surely not where Alice is concerned."

"More with Bev, but don't make me get into it."

"I'll go with you to Portland, if I'm invited. Let's drive there. I've always wanted to see the Pacific Coast. It's a perfect plan. I love to drive, and you've said you love to watch me drive. We can find a bookstore and get some travel guides and maps. You can navigate, and I'll pilot."

"Of course you're invited, but what about your hotel project?"

"I can miss a few days. It's probably a good thing to let Carolyn reestablish herself without me around. I'll check in from the road." Laura walked over to the bed and picked up her hat and gloves. "You sleep on it. Right now, I want a long hot bath and a good night's sleep in a prone position instead of sitting up in an airplane seat. My room is down the hall." Laura fished her room key from her bag. "Room 1421. If you decide on the driving trip, we'll have breakfast and find that bookstore."

Bennie was disappointed Laura wasn't going to stay with her for the night. "You're not still angry?"

"No. It was a misunderstanding, one we could have cleared up on the phone. But if you decide against the driving trip, I'll do some antique shopping. Might as well see if I can find a few special pieces while I'm out here. Sleep tight." She opened the door and was gone.

Chapter Twenty-Three

At breakfast the next morning, they decided on the driving trip and rented a convertible so they'd have a clear view of all the sights. They asked at the hotel desk for the name of a bookstore and found the perfect one down Powell and around the corner from the St. Francis Hotel, off Union Square.

They spent hours sitting on the carpeted floor of the store, browsing through an entire shelf of books and maps about the coastal route from California to Oregon and Washington. On the walk back to the hotel, they took turns carrying the heavy bag of books and pulling each other along the steep grade of Nob Hill. They spent the afternoon and early evening mapping out their route and deciding what sights to see and where they would spend the two nights on the road.

Bennie called her father to tell him she'd be driving to Portland and bringing Laura. She called Alice after dinner.

"She followed you all the way out here? That sounds serious. What about the assistant?"

"I can't talk about her now, but it was all a misunderstanding." Bennie was reluctant to respond more specifically with Laura sitting across the room.

Laura looked up from the travel book she was reading and smiled.

"I called because we're driving to Portland to visit my father. We're leaving tomorrow morning. Thank you so much for the visit, and thanks to Bev too. There's too much to try and say on the phone. I love you. I'll call you from Portland."

"I love you too. Tell Laura I'm expecting her to take good care of you."

Bennie and Laura left early the next morning before the sun had burned away the clouds shrouding the Golden Gate Bridge. As they crossed the bridge and wound upward to Sausalito, Bennie turned in her seat to look out the back window. "Oh, can you look back? The clouds create an illusion the bridge stops in the middle of the Bay. How eerie. It looks like we couldn't go back even if we wanted to." She impulsively kissed Laura on the cheek. "I'm glad we're leaving and that it's just the two of us."

Laura took her hand and kissed her palm. "Didn't you enjoy yourself? Tell me about your visit."

Bennie described Golden Gate Park, their ride on the cable car, and dinner at Bev's house. She told of meeting Dame Renata Glenn and peeking in on the ballet rehearsal.

"Oddly enough, I know her," Laura said. "Small world. She's a good friend of Eva Le Gallienne, the director of American Repertory in New York."

"She mentioned that and offered to introduce me, although she didn't say the name."

"Was Renata making a pass at you? She's rather notorious."

"I can't tell if you're joking or serious." Alice had asked her the same question about Laura.

Laura looked at her with her eyebrows raised.

"She was perfectly nice and was trying to be helpful. We have a lot in common. She has a daughter too."

"Umm-hmm." Laura sounded skeptical.

They drove through Napa Valley, with vineyards stretching to the horizon on both sides of the two-lane blacktop road. They stopped at a turnout to lower the top on the convertible, then turned due west toward the coast highway. As they reached the shore and headed north, they began to see marvelous seascapes of spectacular beauty. The road twisted and turned, hugging the sides of cliffs that dropped to the ocean.

"I'm glad we're driving south to north." Laura shouted over the wind. "It feels safer to be on the inboard side of the road."

The car was substantial and responsive, and before long Laura seemed to capture the rhythm of the road's curves. Bennie gasped at the beauty as each turn revealed a new view. The challenging road made for slow going, but that was offset by the lack of traffic. By the time the sun had risen high enough to peek over the bluffs to the east, they had driven about forty miles.

Laura glanced at the map in Bennie's lap. "How far it is to Tomales Bay? I want to stop when we get there to try some of the local oysters. The book says they're a special treat, not to be missed."

Bennie made a face. "I've never eaten one. Never thought I'd like it. And anyway, raw oysters for breakfast?"

"Pretend you're back home, and it'll be lunch." Laura grinned at her.

The road climbed craggy bluffs, descended to skirt small fishing villages, and rose again. The constant sound of pounding surf against rocks that formed a barrier between the sea and the roadway accompanied them. Laura pointed ahead. "Look. That's Tomales Bay down there. You can see the roofs of the town on the other side. That's where we'll find our oysters."

The highway became Main Street for the old railroad town. To their left, shacks and storefronts lined the Bay, and to their right, wooden false front stores, a clapboard church, and Queen Anne Victorian houses marched up the hillside.

"I have a feeling this is our place." Laura pulled off the highway and into a small parking lot covered in broken shells that crunched under the car's tires. "You don't know it yet, but I have an uncanny talent for being able to pick out the best places to eat by how they look on the outside."

A sign on the roof of the small, whitewashed building proudly pronounced, "Nick's Cove" and underneath "Fresh Tomales Bay Oysters." Inside, Laura and Bennie sat at the Formica counter on red Naugahyde stools. Laura beamed at Bennie. "See? Perfect."

A door behind the counter swung open, and a small man with craggy features came rushing through. His forearms, extending from the sleeves of a pristine white tee shirt, were covered with tattoos. He wore a white sailor hat and a starched white apron that started at his waist and ended at his shoe tops.

"Ladies, welcome to Nick's. That's me." He shook hands with them and looked from one to the other. "What can I get for you? Oysters are the specialty."

"Are they fresh?" Laura asked.

"You bet. Dug 'em myself this morning."

"I'll have a half dozen raw on the half-shell, and she'll try mine before she decides."

"Comin' up."

Nick went back into the kitchen and after a few minutes returned with the plate of oysters resting on a bed of cracked ice. He placed it on the counter in front of Laura, adjusted it until he was satisfied that the plate was situated just right to show off the oysters, and added a saucer of freshly cut lemon wedges and a bottle of hot sauce. He stood back with his hands clasped and waited.

Laura demonstrated for Bennie. "A dot of hot sauce, a squirt of lemon, then swallow. No chewing." She tossed down the oyster. "Lovely," She turned to Bennie. "Now you."

Bennie hesitated and then took a shell and seasoned it as Laura had. She paused an instant and tipped up the shell and swallowed.

Nick and Laura watched Bennie's face.

"What do you think?"

"Not so bad. It smells like the sea and doesn't taste as fishy as I thought. The feeling of it going down is interesting, but I think I'll have some scrambled eggs."

"As you wish." Laura turned her palms up. "You heard the lady, Nick, and another half dozen for me."

Laura tossed down another oyster. "My purpose on this trip is to take your mind off whatever awaits back home. Maybe we can introduce each other to new experiences."

"Oysters and other things too?" Under the counter, Bennie pressed her knee against Laura's and made her smile.

As they left the diner, Bennie pointed out a sandy path leading from the parking lot down to the ocean. "Do we have time to walk a little? My legs could use a stretch."

"I think so."

On the beach, Laura shielded her eyes from the sun and looked up the bluff to the roadway. "We seem to have the place to ourselves."

They slipped off their shoes and walked arm-in-arm along the sand, just out of reach of the surf.

"The guidebook says it's called Hog Island." Bennie pointed toward a brown rock a few hundred feet off the beach. "Though why it's called that, I have no idea. If you look closely, you're supposed to be able to see seals and brown pelicans, but no hogs as far as I can tell."

Laura turned her face toward the breeze blowing in from the sea and closed her eyes with a slight smile on her face.

Bennie touched her lightly on the arm, reluctant to interrupt her reverie. "You look so beautiful and relaxed right now. This trip is good for you too."

Laura nodded.

Bennie threaded her fingers through Laura's hair and kissed her lightly on the lips.

Laura encircled Bennie's wrists with her hands and held her arms behind her back. "What are you doing, Bennie? You asked me to keep our relationship under control, and I will, but you have to cooperate."

"I know." Bennie dug her toes in the sand. "All the trouble seems so far away with just the two of us together in this beautiful spot."

Laura let go of Bennie's arms and sat on the sand. "Sit down here with me." They sat side by side for a while and watched brown pelicans diving for their breakfast. "I want to help you choose your path, not make the choice harder. Get whatever advice you need from whomever. I'll wait."

"You will?"

"Yes, I will."

"What if I don't have any clue what the outcome will be?"

"We'll cross that bridge when we come to it. Right now, as pleasant as this beach is, I think we should get on the road and try and make Mendocino tonight. It's at least another three hours of driving, four if we stop to see the lighthouse at Point Arena." Laura stood up and turned back toward the diner. She began to run, shouting over her shoulder, "Last one to the car is a Tomales oyster."

They drove north along the Sonoma coastline, with placid rangeland and dairy farms to their right and surf boiling against angular cliffs to their left. The road passed through small villages where fishermen were already returning with their day's catch.

At Point Arena, they turned left onto a narrow, windswept peninsula and followed the road lined with misshapen pine trees to the lighthouse. They climbed the one hundred and fifteen feet of stairs to the top. A volunteer guide dressed in nineteenth century sailor garb told them the story of the original lighthouse, built in 1870 and destroyed in the famous 1906 earthquake.

Beyond Point Arena, the landscape changed again. The coast highway perched on cliffs of black volcanic rock that dropped sharply away on the left. Laura had to concentrate on keeping the car as far to the right as possible without scraping the occasional outcroppings. "You can take a nap if you like. I'm fine driving. This road must look even scarier from the passenger seat."

"I'm fine. I'm sorry you have to do all the driving, but you're so much better at it than I am."

As the sun just touched the horizon, Bennie and Laura caught their first view of the red-roofed white and pastel-green houses of Mendocino. South of town, sitting on a promontory of lush green grass, was an eye-catching group of white Victorian buildings with a sign that said Little River Inn. Laura pulled the car into a parking spot in front of the inn and sat for a minute, her forearms and forehead resting on the steering wheel.

"We'll spend the night here. I pushed us too far. I'm worn out. Let's get our room and some supper."

The inn was charming. Their room was on the ground floor facing the ocean with a panoramic view from the two white rocking chairs on the porch. Laura ordered Manhattans from room service and Bennie called her father to report their progress. "We'll be in Oregon tomorrow. Probably make it to Coos Bay for tomorrow night."

"Call me from there. I want to keep track of you on the road. The weather is beautiful here in Portland. I hope the rain holds off while you're here. I can't wait to see you, Bennie, and meet your friend."

"I feel the same. I'm looking forward to some time to talk. I can use your sage advice."

"Is it as I suspected, trouble with Will?"

"That and other things. I'm trying to make sure everything works out the best for Livie."

After she hung up, Bennie went to the porch and sat in the rocker next to Laura. They sipped their drinks and watched the tail-end of the sunset over the ocean—a pink, blue, and grey light show on the horizon. Laura's hand rested on the arm of Bennie's chair, and she rocked them both in unison with the sound of waves breaking below. Driving fatigue overtook Laura, and she dropped off to sleep. Bennie decided to risk trying to get her into her pajamas and in bed so Laura would be rested for the drive the next day. Laura half-woke to help a little, and with a bit of a struggle, Bennie got them both under the covers.

It was still dark when Bennie woke at half past four. She took the telephone into the bathroom and called Livie. Her daughter was full of news about the end of the school year and how she was looking forward to the summer and having more time to spend with Dasher.

"How is your riding instructor, Miss Traynor?"

"Oh, we don't have her anymore. We have Mr. Blake."

Bennie was surprised that Will had made the change. "What happened to Miss Traynor?"

"The other day after our lesson, she told me that I'm doing so good."

"So well, baby."

"So well, and she wants me to be sure and keep learning how to jump, but she thought Daddy and I would be more satisfied with Mr. Blake, so now we have him." Livie chattered on, seeming to have taken the change in stride.

When Bennie hung up and returned to the bedroom, Laura was sitting up, her back propped against the headboard.

"How did you get me into my pajamas? I must have been dead weight."

"You don't remember? You helped."

"How is Livie?"

"Full of news about the end of school and how she plans to spend her summer. I had to coax her to say she misses me."

Laura held the covers up and motioned for Bennie to climb back in bed. "Your hands and feet are freezing. Put your feet under me to warm up. How can California be so cold even in summer?" She wrapped her arms around Bennie and held her close.

"That's an imponderable."

"Here's another imponderable. How can you be so beautiful after crawling out of bed at…" Laura glanced at the bedside clock, "at not even five o'clock in the morning? It's unfair."

"It's inherited. My father is very handsome. When I was a child and he came to visit me in Connecticut, my playmates used to ask me if he was a movie star. I told him that once, and he laughed and said, 'No, I'm just a boring engineer.' He got a faraway look on his face and told me my mother had been very beautiful, and that I would grow up to look like her. He said it is a gift, but not so important as being a good person on the inside. I can still feel him tapping me on the chest, over my heart, when he said that."

"A sweet story. I'm looking forward to meeting your father." Laura gave Bennie a quick hug and padded into the bathroom. "See if room service is awake and order us some coffee and orange juice while I shower and brush my teeth."

They prepared to get back on the road, and while Laura settled their bill, Bennie went with the bellman to load their suitcases in the car. He was a tall, thin young man in his early twenties, dressed in blue jeans and a red windbreaker instead of the more formal uniform of a city hotel.

"I'm Todd."

He managed to hold on to the bags and extend his hand at the same time. He chatted nonstop as they crossed the parking lot, asking Bennie questions about where they were from, where they were headed, and why they were leaving so early, without stopping to enjoy some of the sights in Mendocino. He stowed their luggage in the trunk and walked around the big convertible while Bennie dug in her purse for a tip. He gave an admiring whistle.

"You and your…sister?… have a sweet ride here. I'll bet this baby straightens out the curves fine. I plan to have one like her someday."

"The car's rented, and she's not my sister," Bennie handed him a tip.

"Oh, my mistake. Well, you two have a safe trip."

He patted the hood of the car and ran back across the parking lot.

Chapter Twenty-Four

In the early morning hour, they had the road to themselves. Ten miles north of Mendocino, the road skirted Fort Bragg, then hugged the coast, passing miles of sand dunes and occasional small villages. Then the way turned abruptly inland through dramatic redwood-forested ridges of a mountain range.

Bennie studied the guidebook. "It says these last twenty miles of the coast highway have the sharpest curves and steepest climbs and descents of any other stretch. I'll stay alert and give you moral support." She put her hand on Laura's thigh. "I'm sorry you can't admire the scenery. It's amazing."

After an hour of slow going, the coast highway abruptly ended, merging with busy Route 101 in a nondescript town called Leggett.

Bennie checked the map. "This is anticlimactic. We'll make much better time now, even though it's surely not as scenic. I want to be in Coos Bay before dark if we can. That way we'll have an easy drive into Portland tomorrow. Why don't we stop at a grocery and pick up some food for a quick picnic instead of going in somewhere for lunch?"

"Fine with me." Laura nodded.

It was a three-hour drive to the California-Oregon border and another two and a half hours to Coos Bay. The driving was much easier. Instead of craggy cliffs to their left, the landscape leveled out and they saw miles of sand dunes starting at the edge of the road and obscuring all but an occasional glimpse of ocean. The vegetation changed from redwoods to shore pine and spruce, gnarled by salt spray and wind, growing just above the high-tide mark.

Laura asked Bennie about her father's house and what she remembered of growing up in Portland.

"He still lives in the house they bought when they came to Portland before I was born. I left when I was two years old, but I've been back several times over the years. We took Livie for a visit when she was a baby. She wouldn't remember it."

"Tell me what the house looks like."

"The setting is a hilly part of Portland, so the house has stunning views northeast toward the river. There's a pond and a separate pool house and cottage. The main house has lots of porches and patios. Portlanders love to spend time outdoors." Bennie struggled to re-fold the map properly. When Laura laughed at her, she said, "You can tell this kind of thing is not my strong suit. Ironic since my father is an engineer." She gave up and folded the map in quarters.

"Your father never remarried?"

"No. I think he's had lady friends from time to time, but he keeps that pretty quiet. He and my grandmother have told me many times how well-suited my parents were. I suspect no other woman could live up to his expectations. They must have been a unit and perfectly self-sufficient."

"Where did you fit in?"

"Me?" Bennie thought for a minute. "I was a product of their closeness, and I believe they were loving parents, but I suspect they planned their life, including my place in it, totally focused on each other. When my mother got sick, my father said she had to stay at home instead of traveling with him, but her thoughts were all about getting well for him. Things didn't work out that way."

Laura shook her head. "When you talk about your mother, you sound as though you're telling a story about someone else's life rather than your own."

"It's funny you say that. I've had the same feeling about you when you've told me of your past. Also funny, Will described me the same way when we were arguing about getting a divorce. He said sometimes he expected me to walk out the door and never look back." She picked at a loose thread on her pantleg.

"Away from Livie too?" Laura took her eyes off the road for a quick glance at Bennie.

"That was his implication. Maybe that's partly why he feels so righteous fighting for her. Maybe I've made a terrible mistake staying away from Olivia's and settling for contact with Livie by phone."

Two and a half hours north of the Oregon border, they sighted Coos Bay, so large that the far shore looked like a watercolor painting of distant green lush forests. Golden dunes sometimes obstructed their view of the bay and other times parted to reveal a bustling waterway. In the waning daylight, tugboats guided shipping vessels into and away from the harbor.

Laura said she was worn out from the day's drive, so they stopped at the first decent-looking accommodations on the bayside of the highway. They were delighted with the warm welcome from the young couple who owned the cabins, so new they still smelled of freshly-sawn lumber.

After the proprietor had carried their bags in from the car, Bennie followed him back to the office to call her father. Bennie's call went right through, and her father picked up after the first ring. "Bennie, I've been waiting for you to call."

She was alarmed at the note of concern in her father's voice. Her heart beat faster.

"What is it? Is there something wrong with Livie?" Her stomach tightened. She dreaded the answer.

"No, no, I don't think so. But a telegram from a law firm in New York was delivered for you today. I didn't open it."

"I left your address at Will's office, so it must be from his attorney. Open it, please."

In the seconds she listened to the rustle of her father's opening the telegram, a thousand thoughts crowded Bennie's mind. She was jolted by the fear that Will may have found out she came to visit Alice in California."

"Bennie, do you want me to read it on the phone? Where are you now?"

"We just stopped in Coos Bay. Yes, please read it."

"It says, EXPECT SPECIAL DELIVERY PACKAGE. INFORMATION HAS COME TO LIGHT RE SETTLEMENT. IMPERATIVE YOU RETURN TO NEW YORK IMMEDIATELY."

Bennie grasped at a straw of denial. The ambiguous message could mean anything. The attorneys would be careful to write the telegram that way, except for the part about returning to New York. They were crystal clear about that. They as much as said, "or else."

"Bennie, are you all right?" Her father's voice was anxious. "What can I do?"

"There's nothing to be done tonight. It's just about the troubles between Will and me. As I said, I've been planning to talk to you more about it when we get to Portland. I'm looking forward to getting your advice. Things in New York are speeding up. We'd drive on in tonight, but we're worn out, and it's another four hours."

"Get some sleep and I'll see you tomorrow. Just come as quickly as you safely can."

After they hung up, Bennie made her way along the dark path to their cabin. The moon was just rising, and a cover of clouds blocked what little feeble light would have shone through if the sky had been clear. She could see Laura, framed by a lighted window, kneeling in front of the fireplace to start a fire with the same concentration and intensity with which she approached everything. Bennie stood outside the window in the dark thinking she should never have gotten Laura involved in the mess of her life. She should never have gone to *South Pacific* or to the country club.

Laura turned when Bennie opened the door. "What did your father say? What's the matter? Is it bad news?" She rose from the fireplace.

"Will's lawyer sent a telegram to me at Father's. I'm to expect a special delivery package, and I'm ordered to return East right away."

"What sort of package?" Laura dusted off her hands and skirt. She drew Bennie into the sitting area in front of the fire. "What do they mean right away?"

"It must be a package of legal papers. I think Will found out I was visiting Alice and assumed I'd broken my promise about ending our affair, and now he's filed the divorce papers."

"That's what you've wanted, isn't it?" Laura lit two cigarettes and handed one to Bennie.

"Yes, with all my heart, but if he thinks I've broken our agreement, he may be carrying through with his threat to ask for full custody of Livie. This may be just the excuse he and Olivia needed."

"What did your father say?"

"He said get a good night's sleep and come to Portland as quickly as we can tomorrow."

Laura nodded. "That's good advice. Try not to worry until you get a look at the documents."

Chapter Twenty-Five

They were on the road by sunup the next morning. Laura turned the big convertible away from the coast and headed due east to connect with the highway running up the center of Oregon.

Laura looked over at Bennie. "I hate to leave the beautiful scenery of the coast, but this road is the fastest route to Portland. You can sleep if you want. I know you must be exhausted. You tossed and turned all night."

"I couldn't sleep. Let's have some music." Finding a station with a strong consistent signal proved impossible, and Bennie switched the radio off in frustration. "That's driving me mad."

They stopped at a roadside diner for coffee to go, and once they were back on the road, Laura pressed the gas pedal to the floor. "We've got a straight road and light traffic. Let's see how much distance we can make."

The panicky sensation of being out of control made Bennie want to grip the dashboard. She fought to stay calm and was almost relieved when a highway patrolman pulled them over. Without a word, Laura followed the patrolman back to a small town in order to pay the fine.

A little after noon, they passed a road sign marking the southern Portland city limits, claiming the title, City of Roses. Within sight of downtown, Bennie directed Laura to turn west into an area of steep sloped roads winding through leafy terrain.

"How in the world do you know where we're going? These streets double back on themselves so often, I marvel you keep from getting hopelessly lost."

The houses were set back from the street and represented a mishmash of architectural styles.

"This is the most eclectic neighborhood I've ever seen. When were the houses built?"

"Around 1910, when families first started to have cars. Driving a horse and buggy up these hills must have been tricky. Until they could motor up here, these hillsides were inaccessible for building. We're only ten minutes or so from downtown, but separated by elevation from the more modest neighborhoods, so people could live close to town yet feel exclusive."

Laura pointed out and named the various architectural styles—English Cottage, Foursquare, Colonial, Tudor, Arts and Crafts. "What style is your father's house?"

"You tell me. It's this one on the right."

A white shingled, three-storied, rambling house came into view.

"Cape Cod." Laura turned the big convertible into the steep driveway and pulled to a stop by the front steps.

As they climbed out of the car, Bennie's father opened the front door and bounded down the steps, two red and white Australian Shepherds at his heels. The dogs danced and barked as Bennie's father swept his daughter off her feet in a huge hug. He admonished the dogs. "Settle down, girls. This is Lady and her daughter, Daisy." He petted the dogs' heads. They sat obediently, still squirming with barely contained excitement.

Bennie held on to her father and buried her face in his chest. The two stood together for a long minute before she pulled away, remembering Laura. "Father, this is my special friend, Laura Clayborn."

Bennie's father offered his hand. "Call me Abel, Laura." He encircled each woman's waist. "Let's go right in. I'll get your bags later. Lunch is waiting on the porch. There's a great view of Mt. Hood today. Not a cloud in the sky."

Bennie felt tempted to put off dealing with the telegram and the package for a while, but she knew her mind, and probably Laura's, would be hopelessly distracted until she could measure the extent of the problem she was facing. "Did the package come, Father?"

"Yes, it did. By special messenger first thing this morning. What's this all about, Bennie?" Concern tinged his voice.

"I want to tell you about it when we can sit and focus, but I will say Will and I are talking about a divorce. He's dragging his feet because he wants to stay married, but now, suddenly, when I'm three thousand miles away, something urgent has come up."

"The package and the telegram are on my desk in the study. Laura and I will sit on the porch and get acquainted."

The door to the study was slightly ajar. Bennie stepped into the room and smiled as she surveyed the warm, well-ordered, masculine room that had always been her father's sanctuary. The air held the slightly sweet aroma of her father's pipe. Shelves covered one wall, filled with an eclectic mix of books—philosophy, astronomy, engineering, alongside the latest novels and even a few volumes of poetry. Scattered among the books on the shelves was her mother's collection of Native American baskets and pots. Behind the desk, in front of a bay window, was a stand-up draftsman's table covered with blue-line drawings of an airplane.

In the exact center of the otherwise clean desk was a thick manila envelope stamped SPECIAL DELIVERY with large red letters. She hesitated for a moment before tearing it open. Inside was a divorce petition, filed in Manhattan, with a hearing date set for two weeks.

She scanned the first page and read, "Plaintiff – William Wolff Grant; Defendant – Bennie Elizabeth Grant, Grounds for Divorce – Adultery." She thumbed through the pages to the section about child custody, where she found confirmation of her worst fear. Will was asking for sole legal and physical custody of Livie. Bennie dropped into the desk chair.

"Bennie?" Her father tapped on the door before coming into the room and sitting in a chair in front of the desk.

"Father, thank you for being patient about all this." She looked around the room. "It's comforting just to be here with you. I think I have memories of you sitting at this desk when you and Mother and I all lived here together. That's not possible, is it?"

Abel shook his head.

"I noticed the blueprint you're working on. I thought you'd completely retired from the business."

"They ask for my opinion every once in a while, I think just to humor me."

"Father, I need to talk to you about this divorce business with Will. He and I have both been unhappy in the marriage almost from the beginning." She stopped and tried to think of how to describe the disappointment that had come between them. "We both had expectations of the marriage and each other that didn't happen. He expected me to settle into a role as his wife that completely reflected and complemented him, his family, his social circle, and his business. He didn't want me. He wanted what he could change me into."

"And you? What did you expect?"

"I expected what you and Mother had."

He shook his head. "Your mother and I found each other by accident, probably much the same as you and Will, and it's true over time we grew close as a couple, but our relationship didn't start out that way. We had different temperaments. I can be bull-headed, but your mother was smarter than me. She knew we were best when we valued our differences, instead of trying to change the other. We worked on that as long as we were together."

He stared out the window before going on. "I do have regrets though. I regret we didn't spend more time together as a family, the three of us. I believe we would have come to that, but your mother and I thought we had all the time in the world, and we were building the business together. Life just didn't work out as we had planned."

"I feel so lost, Father."

Abel went around the desk and knelt to embrace her. "I'm so sorry, baby. What about Livie in all this?"

"I thought having Livie would bring Will and me closer together. Instead, it's as though he gave up on me as a lost cause and turned his attention to molding her. I know we both love her and want what's best for her, as we each see it, of course. Agreeing on how to manage that was standing in the way of completing the divorce. Will thought we should stay together, no matter our feelings for each other. His threat was that he'd sue for full custody otherwise, and now he's carrying through with the threat."

Abel raised his eyebrows. "I can't imagine he'll be successful with that...unless there's more than you're telling me."

Bennie searched her heart for the courage to tell her father all of it, about her affair with Alice and her feelings for Laura, but she could not find it. "He can be ruthless getting what he wants. What do you think I should do?" Bennie looked into her father's eyes.

Abel shook his head. "I can't answer that for you, Bennie. I'll just say you're my child, and I want you to be happy. Could you imagine yourself happy in a loveless marriage?"

"No. But won't Livie hate me?"

"However this comes out, stay as close to her as you can, and give her time. She'll come to understand." Abel put his arms around Bennie and rocked her. "How can I help you?"

"I don't even have a lawyer. We've been using Will's to try to work things out amicably, but that's all changed now."

Abel opened a desk drawer and pulled out a leather-bound address book. "I'll get a name of one in your area from my attorney."

As he spoke to his attorney on the phone, Bennie couldn't help smiling, listening to his clear, organized explanation of the reason for his call. He wrote a name and phone number on a sheet of paper. before thanking the attorney and hanging up.

"Jack said this attorney was a classmate, practices in Manhattan, and has exactly the experience and temperament you're looking for. He'll make contact so your call is expected."

Bennie wondered if this attorney could possibly be experienced with a wife and mother wanting to be with her child in spite of having committed adultery with one woman and being involved with another one. Unlikely.

Bennie remembered Laura was sitting on the porch waiting for them. She gave her father a quick hug and led him by the hand out to the sun porch. She sought Laura's eyes and shook her head almost imperceptibly, trying to convey, "Don't ask anything. I'll tell you later."

"Let's have lunch. I'm starved."

After lunch, Abel led them upstairs to adjoining bedrooms with a shared bathroom between. As soon as she was alone, Bennie flopped on the bed and lit a cigarette. She heard a soft knock on the bathroom door. "Come in, Laura."

Laura sat on the side of the bed. "What was in the package?"

"Divorce papers. He filed on grounds of adultery and he's asking for full custody. The hearing is in two weeks. I have to get back to New York right away to meet with a lawyer. Can you believe I don't even have my own lawyer?"

"Do you know why he filed now with you three thousand miles away?"

"He must have found out I was visiting Alice and jumped to the conclusion that she and I were involved again. Something I had promised not to do. The most troubling part is that WIll's not even pretending to be reasonable."

"Does it have anything to do with me?"

Bennie sat up and looked at Laura. "I don't think so. He's focused on Alice and me if you're worried some part of a scandal may rub off on you."

"I wouldn't be too sure. That mother of his doesn't miss a trick. She certainly looked me up and down at the country club, and she may have picked up on my snide purpose in writing that note I left her. My intuition is that she has had struggles of her own, maybe even with the same issues as yours."

"I've suspected that too." Bennie looked down at her hands. "Are you afraid being associated with me will blemish your character?"

Laura picked up a China figurine from the nightstand and turned it in her hand. "Charles and I have maintained a façade of a normal married couple, but I've always thought my sexual preferences were nobody's business but mine. At the same time, I've known that people, and I'm talking about both businesspeople and society in general, fear what they don't understand. When I met Charles at the beginning of my business career we became close friends, soulmates really. He and I both thought getting married would be a solution, a way of not having to explain or make excuses."

"Have you had long-term relationships with women?"

"If you mean have I lived with a woman and excluded Charles, no, and neither has Charles presented me with any rivals, if you want to look at it that way. It's part of our unspoken pact. I've had periods of monogamy with some women. I suppose you might call me a serial monogamist." Laura smiled ruefully at her own joke.

"Have you been satisfied with that?"

"As long as the woman in question was satisfied, I suppose I was." Laura placed the figurine back on the bedside table. She took Bennie's face in her hands and gently traced her cheekbones with her fingertips. "Let's get you back home and through this next part."

Chapter Twenty-Six

Bennie was early for her appointment with the attorney, so she had the taxi driver drop her in front of the arch where Fifth Avenue dead-ended at Washington Square Park in Greenwich Village. The weather was beautiful, not yet deep enough into summer to bring oppressive heat and humidity to the city. She strolled into the park and stood watching children, many of them around Livie's age, splashing in the fountain while their mothers reclined around the fountain's edge and chatted with one another. Two old men sat at a chessboard, deep in concentration, as a teenage boy watched.

She walked west along the street bordering the north edge of the park until she stood in front of a red brick, three-story town house. She checked the name and address on the slip of paper her father handed her just three days ago in his study in Portland, *August Mapes, 26 Washington Square North.* The building wasn't anything like the concrete and steel high-rise on Wall Street where she and Will met with his attorney. She climbed the steps and read a brass plate beside the front door with the simple legend, August Mapes, Attorney at Law. She was in the right place.

The door opened to a small foyer. On the right was a reception and waiting area which, in the nineteenth century, was a formal parlor. A secretary looked up from her typewriter.

"Mrs. Grant?"

"Yes."

"Please be seated, and we'll be with you in just a moment."

Bennie leafed through a magazine without really focusing. She was too nervous to concentrate. After a few minutes, she heard a door open across the foyer. A woman strode into the waiting room. She was tall and slim and wore a tailored suit with a starched white cotton blouse. Her hair and eyes were a rich shade of brown that on a fine piece of furniture would be called mahogany, and there was grey at the temples, which the woman made no effort to hide.

"Mrs. Grant, I'm August Mapes." She shook hands with Bennie. "This way, please."

Without waiting for a reply from Bennie, the lawyer headed across the foyer to her office. When they were seated, she picked up a file from her desk and opened it. "Sorry for the wait. I was speaking with your husband's attorney."

Even though the file was upside down to her, Bennie could see it contained the divorce papers with August's neat, handwritten notes in the margins. "Now, Mrs. Grant, before we get into the details of your case, let's start with any questions you have for me."

"You're a woman," Bennie blurted out. The comment was so incongruous that both Bennie and August laughed.

"Yes, I am. The name threw you off. I get that often." Miss Mapes gestured to the framed diploma on the wall behind her. "If you want to know my qualifications, I graduated first in my class at Yale, was Law Review there for my last two years, and before coming out on my own, I was an associate at Shearman and Sterling."

"Why did you decide to go on your own?"

"I graduated law school and passed the New York bar when our country was getting into the war in earnest. When Pearl Harbor happened, all the men went off to serve, and the law firms had no choice but to hire women. The partners at Shearman made it abundantly clear there was no promotion in my future, so I left. It's worked out for the best. I like being my own boss. Anything else?"

"Can you help me fight for custody of my daughter?"

"I believe I can. Your husband is taking a radical step asking that a little girl be kept away from her mother. His attorney is making some veiled allusions to a morals argument. Perhaps you can fill me in on the details. I'll be better able to give you an answer to what our approach might be. The grounds in the divorce filing is adultery. Does your husband have evidence of you having relations with someone outside your marriage?"

"Yes." Bennie tried to settle more comfortably into her chair, anticipating this could be a long and difficult conversation.

"What evidence?" August's eyes were focused on the pen she held over a yellow legal tablet as she asked this question, and she didn't look up. Bennie was glad August was trying to approach the questions as discreetly as possible.

"I told him. It was foolish I know, but he was badgering me about why I wanted a divorce."

"Does he know whom you had the relationship with?" August looked up at her.

"Yes, I told him that too. The person was my best friend." Bennie hesitated. "A woman."

August nodded. She set her pen on the desk, lining it carefully up with the edge of the tablet. She listened without interrupting as Bennie told of her unhappiness in the marriage and of her affair with Alice.

"And you're not involved with her now?"

"Not in that way, but she remains my best friend. I was visiting her in San Francisco when Will filed for divorce."

"Was she ever around your daughter?"

"Of course. She was at the hospital when Livie was born and has always been a part of our lives. Livie loves her like an aunt."

August went back to making notes on the legal pad. "Are you involved with anyone now?"

Bennie wasn't sure how to answer that question. She could say no since she and Laura had not been intimate since that day at the country club, but if Will found out about Laura and that they were in California together, he could use it against her in court and blindside her attorney. She settled on a half answer. "Not exactly involved, but there is a woman that I'm interested in."

August nodded. "I see. Does your husband know about your interest in this other person?"

Bennie shook her head. "I don't think so."

The lawyer asked Bennie about the details of her marriage to Will. Were there arguments? Was there ever physical violence? Did Livie see or hear her parents argue?

She asked about the year they were separated. Why did Bennie agree to Livie's staying with Will at his mother's? How often did she visit Livie? She also asked about her financial situation, where she was living, and whether she had a job.

The more questions August asked, the more Bennie's spirits sank. She saw how the path she had taken, trying to placate Will and get him to agree to an amicable divorce and to share custody of Livie would appear she was shirking her responsibilities as a mother.

"Mrs. Grant, would you like some water or some tea?"

Bennie looked up. August's face was lined with concern.

"No, I'm…it seems so hopeless when I hear myself try and explain things."

"It's not hopeless. I can begin to see a way forward. Let's stop for today. You and I both have homework. I'll prepare a response to the divorce papers. It's pretty routine. I'll ask for a month's continuance, which gives us about five weeks to get up to speed. Your husband has asked you be prohibited from contacting your daughter until the hearing. I believe our response can successfully argue that's unduly harsh, though frankly, the more unreasonable he sounds, the better for us. In the meantime, you need to find a permanent place to live and a job. We need to be able to show you have a plan for the future with your daughter. You should not see this woman you're interested in. Your husband may be having you followed. And do not contact your friend in California."

How can I survive the next few weeks without Alice's support and not talking to Laura?

August reached into her desk drawer, pulled out a business card, and placed it on the desk in front of Bennie. "This next part is difficult, and what you choose to do is entirely up to you. This is the name and number of a psychiatrist. You may want to start seeing her during the time before the hearing, both for support and because the judge will view your action as evidence you are working on your problem, as he may see it."

Bennie was stunned. "You're saying that in order to be a part of my daughter's life I have to pretend to be working on curing myself from some mental disease."

"Believe me, I understand your reaction. I'm trying to offer you my best advice on our building the strongest case. As I said, it's entirely your choice."

Bennie picked up the card and after looking at it for a moment, dropped it in her purse.

Chapter Twenty-Seven

Back in her hotel room, Bennie sat at the desk to write Alice a letter.

Dearest,

> *Much has happened in the last week. Will filed divorce papers in Manhattan I'm sure to try and spare his friends in New Canaan the scandal he anticipates from our lurid story. He's using adultery as grounds and he means you and me. I'm so sorry you may be drawn into this. He's asking for full custody of Livie and will try to keep her completely away from me. My father steered me to an attorney that I've come from meeting for the first time. She, yes, she, is awfully smart, and I feel somewhat optimistic that if we have a chance, she'll find it.*

> *Her advice is that I not be in contact with you for the next few weeks, probably five weeks. I can hardly stand to think about not having your steady influence and support, but I guess that's the reality of the situation.*

> *As soon as I can, I'll call you. I'm staying at the Pierre and will be looking for an apartment here in Manhattan.*

All my love, Bennie

Before starting a second letter, to Laura, Bennie fished in her purse for cigarettes and her hand brushed the psychiatrist's business card August had given her. She pulled it out, looked from the phone number on the card to the telephone sitting on the desk, shook her head, and dropped the card back in her purse.

Dear Laura,

> *I've been to see the attorney Father recommended. August Mapes is a very attractive and competent woman. She grilled me thoroughly about what Will might have up his sleeve. I've come away feeling the next few weeks, about five weeks if the judge grants the continuance she's*

going to ask for, will be a challenge, especially since she says I must stay away from you in case Will is having me followed. I hate to think he would stoop to that, but Miss Mapes seemed to think it's a possibility. I know you'll understand. She's given me what she calls homework that will keep me occupied—finding an apartment and a job.

You asked me once why I've been marching in place instead of working toward my passion to be a director. My reaction when you asked was to feel judged by you. You didn't seem to understand about my struggle with Will and my concern about Livie, but now I know I was being defensive. It's time for action. I'm going to find a job in the theater, no matter if it's as an assistant to an assistant.

As soon as I've found an apartment, I'll get my things from your guesthouse and leave your key and a note with my new address. I'll miss you. I hope you meant what you said on the beach, and that you won't give up on me as a lost cause.

Bennie

The next week, Bennie found a two-bedroom apartment on East 63rd Street. The bedroom she thought of as Livie's had a large window looking out over a courtyard area at the back of the building, with trees and a small square of grass. They would choose the colors for the walls and curtains together, and they might even paint the bedroom themselves.

August Mapes called with the news that the judge granted a continuance and set the hearing date in six weeks. He also ordered that Bennie be allowed to speak with Livie on the phone in the meantime. Bennie took this as a good sign.

"And there's something else. Mr. Bell says that Will wants to meet with you."

"What about?"

"Bell says it's against his advice, but Will wants to explain in person why he's going for full custody of Livie."

"Do you think I should meet with him?"

August paused. "As your attorney, it's hard for me to see how such a meeting would help our case. He may want to assuage his conscience about taking a little girl away from her mother, but I doubt he'll change his position. As a woman, if I were you, I'd want to take a last chance to try and change his mind, and he might reveal some clues about the tack they plan to take in court. I think we have a good, strong argument for joint custody, but there are no guarantees how the judge will see the facts. On balance, I don't see a down-side to your meeting with him."

"Tell them I'll meet with Will."

* * *

Bennie and Will arranged to meet at the Palm Court in the Plaza Hotel on Saturday. As Bennie walked down Fifth Avenue to Central Park South, carriage drivers coaxed their sleepy horses into line, awaiting customers for a ride through the park. Traffic on Fifth Avenue was light, unlike the moving sea of yellow cabs that would already be flowing at this hour during a weekday. The taxis honked and darted from lane to lane, as if unable to break nervous habits developed during rush-hour traffic.

The doorman touched the bill of his hat and smiled as he held the front door of the Plaza open for Bennie. The Palm Court was filled with the afternoon tea crowd. Bennie was on time, but Will hadn't arrived. The maître d' showed Bennie to a small table, and she chose the seat facing the entrance so she could see Will coming and prepare herself. As she waited, she remembered Will told her once that his habit was to arrive early to a business meeting, and to stand hidden off to the side while his adversary arrived so that he could observe anything that might give him the advantage. She looked around the room, lined with potted palm trees where Will might be skulking but didn't see him. She went to the ladies' room, and when she came back, Will was sitting at the table.

He rose and held her chair. "Hello, Bennie. You look wonderful. You're always the most beautiful woman in the room."

The waiter took their orders, tea for Bennie and scotch on the rocks for Will. When they had their drinks, Will said, "You haven't seen Livie ride lately. She's getting better every week with her jumping. I may have to get her a bigger horse soon."

"Livie told me Janice Traynor isn't her instructor any longer."

Will sipped his drink. "Yes, Janice decided another instructor might be better."

"I thought things were going so well with her. I thought you might be interested in Janice personally."

Will laughed. "Yes, well, it turned out Janice would have been more likely to be interested in you than in me."

Bennie set her teacup down so hard it made the saucer rattle. "Can we get to the point? Why are we meeting, Will?"

"Do we have to start off this way?" Will leaned across the table and lowered his voice. "Can't we have a civilized discussion in pleasant surroundings about our daughter and her future?"

"When you're taking me to court to assure that I never see her?" Bennie shook her head. "You are unbelievable."

"We had a deal, and you violated it. Do you think this is the way I want things to go? I've told you…" A man passing their table recognized Will, stopped to shake his hand, and moved on.

Will turned back to Bennie. "I wanted to meet and convince you that we don't have to go to court and air our dirty laundry in front of a bunch of strangers. I'd like you to consider that Mother and I can give Livie the best life. I'm willing, and Mother is too, to have you in our home whenever you like."

"Livie should be living with me half the time. How confused will she be having a mother who visits her occasionally?"

"How confused will she be with a mother who has unnatural so-called friendships with other women?"

Bennie picked up her purse and gloves and pushed her chair back from the table. "We're getting nowhere. I should have known better than to think we might find some common ground. I'm leaving."

Will signaled the waiter. "At least let me get the check and put you in a taxi." He paid the bill and took Bennie's arm as they left the hotel.

The doorman blew his whistle to signal a taxi.

Will stuffed his hands in his pockets. "This isn't ending the way it should."

"I know. Goodbye, Will."

Chapter Twenty-Eight

Bennie combed the newspapers for information about plays starting production and announcements of casting calls. Every day she made a circuit of the Broadway theater district, sitting in the back rows of dark auditoriums until a break when she could approach each stage manager or director to inquire about a position as an assistant or general gofer. After two weeks of sometimes polite but more often gruff rejections, she decided to contact Renata Glenn about her friend who might have something. Bennie chanced calling the theater in San Francisco and took it as a good omen when Renata came on the line right away.

"Of course I'll put in a word for you with my dear friend, Eva Le Gallienne. As I'm sure you know, she's quite a ubiquitous actress on Broadway, though lately she's been producing and directing. I've heard she's currently working on a revival of *The Children's Hour* at the Coronet Theater. I'll call her right away. I'm sure she'll see you. You'll find her very simpatico. Be sure and mention my name."

Bennie hurried to a bookstore for a copy of *The Children's Hour* and spent all evening reading and re-reading the play. The next morning, at ten o'clock sharp, she arrived at the Coronet Theater. She tiptoed down the aisle in the darkened theater and took a seat a few rows behind three men and a woman. She assumed the woman was Eva Le Gallienne. Auditions were in full swing for the role of young Mary Tilford, the character whose whispered lie brings ruin to the two boarding school owners.

As each hopeful actress was called forward to read, an assistant with a clipboard asked some questions about previous experience and training, then told her to read lines. Each time, Le Gallienne leaned over to whisper to the assistant, who said, "Thank you. We'll let you know. Next." Another assistant, backstage, brought out the next candidate.

How did Le Gallienne make up her mind so quickly?

After about an hour, Le Gallienne stood and stretched. The assistant with the clipboard went to the stage and spoke to the aspiring actresses who were still waiting to audition.

"That's all for today. We'll see you tomorrow, same time."

Le Gallienne turned toward the back of the theater and saw Bennie.

"Are you here to read?" Her accent was an unusual mix of her native England and New York stage. "If so, you're in the wrong place. We're casting young Mary today."

Bennie rose and went forward with her hand extended.

"Miss Le Gallienne, I'm Bennie Grant. I believe Renata Glenn spoke to you about me."

The director's short, brown hair was casually styled. She wore a man-tailored gabardine suit. She looked puzzled for a moment, and then appeared to remember. "Ah, yes. Dame Renata mentioned you'd be coming around." She used the dancer's formal title with a lilt in her voice. Le Gallienne cocked her head, and Bennie felt her keen gaze size her up in an instant. "I'm sorry. I'm running off right now, but here's my address. Come by the apartment around five, can you?"

She took the clipboard from her assistant's hand, wrote an address on the bottom of the page, ripped it off, and handed it to Bennie. "See you at five."

Bennie left the theater excited and hopeful. The way Le Gallienne looked and spoke to her gave her reason to be optimistic that the director would make a place for her in the production. To take up the time until her appointment, she had lunch at a diner across the street from the theater and afterward found a bench in Central Park where she sat and read *The Children's Hour* again. She tried to discern what Le Gallienne was looking for in the part of Mary Tilford that she hadn't found in the morning's casting call.

She rang the bell outside Le Gallienne's apartment at exactly five o'clock. The director herself answered the door. Le Gallienne drew her into the apartment and guided her into a cozy living room with large windows facing Central Park. Another woman, about Le Gallienne's age, was sitting on the sofa, her feet tucked underneath her, sipping a cocktail. Over the fireplace was a portrait of Eva Le Gallienne in the role of Peter Pan.

"Thank you for seeing me, Miss Le Gallienne."

"Call me Eva, and this is my companion, Marion Evensen. Marion, this is Bennie Grant, Renata's friend."

Marion acknowledged the introduction with a little wave and a smile.

"As you see, Bennie, we're having drinks. What can I get for you?"

"A Manhattan?"

"How is Renata, and how do you know her?" Eva asked once they were settled with their drinks.

"I met her in San Francisco at a friend's dinner party. She's guest dance mistress this season with the San Francisco Ballet, but I'm sure you know that."

"What Eva is really fishing for, Bennie," Marion drawled, "is how well you know her. Renata implied very well, but one can't always trust her implication."

"As I said, I met her at a dinner party in San Francisco, and we hit it off. She generously offered an introduction to you when she heard of my interest in the theater."

Eva exchanged a look with Marion. "Renata always has a keen eye for potential, but now you can speak for yourself without depending on Renata. How can I help you?"

"Let me work on *The Children's Hour*. I'll do anything." Bennie tried hard not to sound desperate.

Eva nodded. "I sympathize with you, trying to get started. I was fifteen and exceedingly lucky since I had no training. I started as an actor. You have no interest in that? You certainly have the looks."

"I want to be a director. It's all I've ever wanted to do."

Eva placed a cigarette in an ebony holder, lit it, and fixed Bennie with an intense stare. Tell me what you think *The Children's Hour* is about."

"It's about the power of a lie to do evil."

Eva smiled. "Not about lesbianism?"

Bennie's heart sank. Her chance to work with Eva might rest on her answer to this question. The only thing she knew to do was to plough forward. "I don't think the author meant the play to be about lesbianism. In fact, when it was made into a movie, twenty years ago, Miss Hellman rewrote the screenplay to be about a false accusation of a relationship between a man and a woman, to get the script past the review board. She hardly changed any of the dialogue."

Eva smiled and nodded. "But today, in 1951, do you think the ending makes sense without the lesbian theme? Martha killing herself?"

Bennie shook her head. "I don't think the ending makes sense at all."

Eva raised her eyebrows. "Do you think we should press Miss Hellman to let us have Karen and Martha live happily ever after?"

"Would she do that?"

Eva glanced at Marion again. "No, she won't. She's concerned about the commercial success of this production. She sees it as an important statement against the travesty going on right now with Mr. McCarthy's hearings in Washington. She doesn't want to shock the public's sensibilities with a happy ending. It could turn them off from coming to see the play. But I think we can make this production about a particular lie that has the consequence of spoiling something simple, natural, and beautiful. That's my vision anyway. We'll see how the public responds."

Bennie held her breath, waiting for what would come next. She listened to the steady ticking of a grandfather clock in the hallway. Eva made a decision about Bennie as quickly as she had made up her mind against the girls trying out for the role of Mary.

"I think we can squeeze you in. The salary is only thirty dollars a week. Will that do?"

Bennie leaned forward. "Yes, yes."

"Perfect. Be at the theater at nine tomorrow morning."

Marion held up her glass in a toast, gazing at Eva. "Here's to happy endings."

Chapter Twenty-Nine

The smell of freshly brewed coffee filled Eva Le Gallienne's tiny backstage office. Bennie made the coffee by touch rather than turning on the lights in the windowless space, hoping to spare Miss LeG, as the director preferred to be called, some small amount of the heat that would make the room stifling as the day wore on. Brewing the day's first pot of coffee, strong and black, was the beginning of Bennie's job every day, seven days a week, for the last month.

She was grateful for the activity and the intense pace of putting together a Broadway opening. The job kept her too busy to worry about her upcoming court date or to dwell on thoughts of Laura. Even though Bennie was clear in her letter that her attorney thought their seeing each other would be unwise, she was disappointed Laura made no move to get in touch with her.

This morning, Bennie was rushing to set up a large table with fourteen chairs near the front of the stage. The casting was complete and that day would be the first table reading of the script, when the ensemble of actors came together and read the play aloud in their roles for the first time. The run-through would be the director's and the cast's first opportunity to hear the text spoken.

Patricia Neal was to play Martha. The actress, better known for her movie roles, was a favorite of the producer, Kermit Bloomgarden, and the author of the play, Lillian Hellman. Miss Neal had made her stage debut in another Hellman play, *Another Part of the Forest*, for which she won a Tony Award. Bennie supposed Miss Neal appealed to Mr. Bloomgarden's accountant temperament as a good financial risk, and to Miss Hellman's sense that she could interpret her work well. At her audition, Neal read for both main characters, Martha and Karen. Mr. Bloomgarden gave her the choice of either part, and she chose Martha. Bennie thought the choice of the lesbian character was a brave one for Neal, and she was anxious to see how the actress interpreted the role.

The other main character, Karen, would be played by Kim Hunter. If Miss LeG were right that Lillian Hellman wanted this revival of her play, about the power of an evil lie to destroy innocent people, to make a statement about the damage being done by Senator McCarthy's House

Unamerican Activities Committee, Bennie found this casting choice deliciously ironic. Kim Hunter was blacklisted in Hollywood for being suspected of belonging to the Communist Party.

The most difficult part to cast had been Mary Tilford, the student who whispers to her grandmother an accusation of an illicit relationship between the two headmistresses. Twenty actresses read for the part before Eva Le Gallienne finally chose a relatively inexperienced twelve-year-old, Iris Mann. Bennie's job, between bringing Miss LeG endless cups of coffee and emptying overflowing ashtrays, was to read the grandmother's dialogue for each aspiring Mary to play against. After the first page of Iris' reading, Miss LeG's voice rang out from the front of the auditorium. "That's enough."

The assistant director bounded onto the stage and pumped the girl's hand. "You're our Mary. Congratulations."

When she got the opportunity, Bennie asked the assistant director to explain the choice. He shrugged his shoulders. "I don't ask many questions, but she did lean over to me and whisper, 'Watch how she can make herself appear dead around the eyes when she tells the lie.' Miss LeG said she'd seen that same look on Joe McCarthy's face."

As Bennie prepared for the table read, laying out scripts with each character's name neatly printed on the front, she replayed in her mind her phone call with Livie that morning, full of her daughter's chatter about her friends at school and her jumping lessons. Bennie called at eight o'clock every weekday morning. She and the butler had settled into a routine that assured his putting Livie on the phone directly, without Bennie having to speak to Olivia. Bennie assumed Olivia was probably as happy avoiding speaking as she was. Bennie supposed their confrontation would come soon enough in the courtroom.

Bennie arranged the principal characters' scripts near the head of the table with secondary characters spread down the length of the table. She worried over whether to put Patricia Neal or Kim Hunter at the head of the table. She decided to leave the head empty and to put their scripts across from each other. She placed pitchers of water and glasses in several spots and stood back with her hands folded to check her work.

Both the producer and playwright were expected to attend this first run through, and Bennie could sense an electricity of anticipation in the air as actors and crew arrived. Even Miss LeG seemed jumpy the evening before, lighting one cigarette off another and giving Bennie the same instructions over and over. She was showing her nerves about scrutiny from the producer or the playwright or both.

Actors took their seats, most of them leafing through their copies of the play and marking their parts. The rest chatted in groups of twos or threes. Everyone turned in unison when the doors in the back of the auditorium swung open to let in sunlight and the three principles of the morning—author, producer, and director. Le Gallienne and Bloomgarden took seats in the third row and Hellman stayed at the back of the auditorium, smoking and pacing back and forth behind the last row of seats.

Miss LeG greeted the actors. "We'll read all the way through without stopping. If you stumble, never mind, keep reading. We're going to start getting used to the play's tempo."

Far from stumbling, the two stars had already memorized their parts and, during the two-hour reading, delivered the lines with passion and authenticity. At the end of the last act, everyone around the table stood and applauded. Neal and Hunter embraced each other across the table.

Miss LeG joined in the applause. "Splendid, splendid. We'll take a fifteen-minute break and then go through Act One again".

Mr. Bloomgarden came to the stage and shook hands with Patricia Neal and Kim Hunter. Miss LeG called Iris over for a quiet conversation.

Standing in the wings, Bennie shaded her eyes with her hand and squinted into the darkness to gauge Lillian Hellman's reaction. Instead of the author, who had apparently slipped out of the theater sometime during the reading, Bennie saw Laura sitting in the last row.

Bennie ran up the aisle and led Laura into a tiny coat check room off the deserted lobby. They sat on two spindly metal folding chairs. "How in the world did you find me? I seem to ask that question often."

"Your husband isn't the only one who can have you followed, you know. And, by the way, he is having you followed. There's a guy in a grey fedora sitting at the end of the counter in the diner across the street. I suspect he waits there every day."

"Good." Bennie raised one slat of the venetian blind covering a small window to peek at the front of the diner. "I hope Will is wasting lots of money on him. I do nothing but work, sleep, and talk to Livie on the phone every morning."

Laura pulled Bennie into her lap and kissed her. "My bigshot director. I've missed you."

Bennie felt a stirring in the pit of her stomach. She had been too busy to think of anything but the play, but right now she could think of nothing but the warmth and softness of Laura's lips. She reluctantly pulled away. "I have to go back."

"I know. I shouldn't have bothered you, but I knew Le Gallienne was doing the table reading today, and I wanted to give you moral support, if you needed it. Looks like you don't, but it appears Miss Hellman could use some."

"What do you mean?"

"She paced back and forth and muttered through the whole reading. Finally, she mumbled, 'I need a drink.' and stalked out."

"Miss LeG said Miss Hellman is unable to sit through the performance of her plays. She has a lot at stake with this production. How did you know about the table reading?"

"Charles knows everything that goes on in the theater in this town. What about your divorce? Can you use moral support for that?"

"Next Wednesday is the day we go to court for the first and, I hope, the last time. August says we're ready. She's helped me practice by grilling me as Will's lawyer probably will. We'll be in front of Judge Stone. August said he goes by the book, but he's fair." Bennie stood with her hand on the doorknob but made no move to open it. "My affair with Alice is our vulnerability, now that I am settled in a job and an apartment. She says we'll answer those questions truthfully and focus on how I've rehabilitated myself. Isn't that dreadful?"

"Yes. Will there be other people in the courtroom?"

"Olivia is named on Will's witness list. She's always behind Will. Has been through this whole thing. Probably no one else though." Bennie opened the door a crack. "I need to go. Miss LeG is already extending herself to let me be away from rehearsal next week."

Laura pushed the door closed again. "I know. One more kiss. You can telephone me after court, right?" She embraced Bennie and kissed her.

Chapter Thirty

"All rise." The bailiff's voice echoed through the almost-empty courtroom, off the marble floors and the twenty-foot polished wood ceiling. Will and his attorney and Bennie and August rose in unison as the judge came through a door behind the raised platform and took his seat.

"Court is now in session, the Honorable Francis Stone presiding."

The butterflies in Bennie's stomach stirred, and she had to hold on to the table in front of her to keep from losing her balance. August smiled reassuringly and mouthed, "It's okay."

The court clerk, seated to the judge's left stood and faced Bennie and Will. "Raise your right hands. Do you swear to tell the truth, the whole truth, and nothing but the truth, so help you God?"

"I…" Bennie had to clear her throat to get out the second word. "Do."

"Be seated."

Bennie peeked over her shoulder at the empty seats behind Will and Mr. Bell, surprised to see Olivia was not there.

The judge opened a file in front of him. "Mr. Bell, your client Mr. William Grant is petitioning this court for a divorce from his wife on grounds of adultery."

"Yes, Your Honor."

"And Miss Mapes, your client, Mrs. Grant, has responded that she is in agreement with the terms of the petition regarding dissolution of the marriage and distribution of assets and property, including that there will be no ongoing spousal support from Mr. Grant to Mrs. Grant. However, she is not in agreement with Mr. Grant's request for sole physical custody of their daughter." The judge referred to the file. "Olivia Elizabeth Grant."

"That's correct, Your Honor."

The judge removed his glasses and rubbed his eyes. "Before we begin with the Petitioner's case, I want to get some things clear, Mr. and Mrs. Grant. In spite of what you may have seen in the movies, I'm not in the business of solving your problems. I'm in the business of making decisions based on facts. My job is to listen to all the evidence your able attorneys present, and to decide, as fairly as possible, who wins and who loses. Thank goodness, most people who can't make their marriages work come to agreements about the terms of this failure without having to bring their disputes before the court.

"However, sometimes, as in your case, they can't agree. This is the worst example of that. When I spoke of winners and losers, I was not referring to just the two of you. There will be one sure loser resulting from this argument you are about to have in a public courtroom, and that is your daughter. Over the next few hours, you'll say very hurtful things about each other, doing terrible damage to the ongoing relationship you must continue in some form as the parents of this little girl, and that will fall on her shoulders."

Bennie clasped her hands in her lap. *Could it be true that by fighting for Livie I risk hurting her?*

The judge went on. "Whatever is driving you—pride, anger, resentment, self-righteousness—I want to know before we begin that you are certain you cannot agree. Mr. Grant?"

"Yes, Your Honor, I'm certain."

"Mrs. Grant?"

"Yes."

The judge shook his head and put his glasses back on. "Off we go then. Mr. Bell, carry on."

Will's attorney pushed his chair back and rose. "Your Honor, I call to the stand Mr. William Grant."

Will climbed the two steps to the witness box and focused his eyes on his attorney, avoiding any eye contact with Bennie.

The clerk stood again. "State your full name and your address."

"William Wolff Grant. 677 South Avenue, New Canaan, Connecticut."

Mr. Bell walked to a podium between the two tables and opened a folder. "Mr. Grant, how long have you and your wife been married?"

"Nine and a half years."

"Would you say that in some part of that time your marriage was happy?"

"Yes, most of it, up until about a year ago."

"Up until a year ago. What were the indications that made you feel your marriage was happy?"

Will glanced at Bennie before answering. "We had a nice home in a pleasant town. We had Livie, of course, who is bright and healthy. My business is going well, growing every year, and it provided us with every material thing we needed. We had friends. We had the club."

"You mentioned friends. Was Alice Gifford one of Mrs. Grant's friends?"

"Yes, Bennie and Alice have been best friends since they were children."

"How often did Mrs. Grant see Miss Gifford?"

"To my direct knowledge, at least once or twice a week."

"Was your daughter ever present when Mrs. Grant and Miss Gifford were together?"

"Yes, Livie often told me about her day over dinner, and she often described the two of them, Bennie and Livie, being in the company of Alice."

Mr. Bell paused, reorganized the papers in front of him on the podium, and went on. "Did you and your wife have regular marital relations, Mr. Grant?"

"Yes."

"During this happy time in your marriage, up until a year ago, did Mrs. Grant express dissatisfaction with your marriage?"

"We had normal disagreements from time to time. She wanted to become active in the amateur theater group in New Canaan. At first, I was concerned it might take too much of her time from Livie, but Bennie went ahead with her plans anyway."

"What happened a year ago, when your marriage became not so happy?"

"We had been to a Fourth of July party at the country club, and we got home late. Bennie came into my bedroom as I was undressing for bed and announced, out of the blue, that she wanted a divorce."

"And what was your response, Mr. Grant?"

"I was aghast. Shocked. I asked her why. She said she had found something she needed outside our marriage and that she wanted not to be married to me anymore. I didn't understand what she meant, so I pressed her for more details. That's when she told me she had been having a love affair with Alice Gifford."

"Where was your daughter during this time?"

"Livie had left the club party early with my mother, her grandmother, after the fireworks display, and she was spending the weekend there, with my mother."

"What happened after Mrs. Grant told you about her affair?"

"I told Bennie I wanted her out of the house, and she packed a bag and left."

"Where are you living now, Mr. Grant?"

"Since July of last year, Livie and I have been living with my mother in New Canaan."

"And is your daughter in school?"

"She's in third grade at Country Day School in New Canaan, where she's attended since kindergarten."

Bennie had been dreading this line of questions about the particulars of their daughter's situation and the impact their separation had on her. She swallowed hard to maintain her composure. August patted her hand under the table and wrote in the margin of her legal tablet, *Don't worry. We'll have our turn.*

Mr. Bell cleared his throat. "Mr. Grant, would you say your daughter is successful at Country Day School? Does she enjoy going there?"

Will smiled for the first time since he took the stand. He glanced again at Bennie. "She does very well." His pride was evident in his voice. "She makes good marks, and she has lots of friends."

"And does she have other interests, outside of school?"

"I got her a pony for Christmas, and she is training to jump."

"Where does Livie do this training?"

"My mother's home has stables and a riding arena."

Mr. Bell rearranged his papers again. Bennie suspected this was a ploy to let the picture of a happy and well-adjusted little girl sink into the judge's mind before going on. "Mr. Grant, does your wife have contact with your daughter?"

"Yes, we often have dinner together at my mother's, and Bennie, Mrs. Grant, comes to watch Livie's riding lessons. I believe she regularly calls Livie before her school day starts. I've usually left for the city by that time."

"Would you say those times that you have dinner together are amicable?"

"Yes, I would say that both Bennie and I are careful to keep any discord away from our daughter." Will looked at Bennie and held her gaze. "I know we both love our daughter very much."

"Why, then, Mr. Grant, are you requesting sole physical custody of your daughter?"

Will looked away from Bennie. "I do not believe Bennie can provide the proper home environment for our daughter. She has admitted to having an unnatural relationship with a woman, whom she persists in keeping company with, and I believe it is my responsibility as a parent to protect my daughter from influences such as those."

"Thank you, Mr. Grant. No more questions at this time, Your Honor."

August patted Bennie's hand again and rose to stand behind the podium. "Good morning, Mr. Grant."

"Good morning."

"Mr. Grant, you stated that, up until last July fourth, your marriage was happy."

"That's right."

"Up until last July, did your wife, Mrs. Grant, work outside the home?"

"No. She did charity work from time to time, but she was a full-time mother for our daughter."

"You describe your daughter as being healthy and bright and successful in school."

"Yes, very much so."

"Would you say Livie and Mrs. Grant have a close relationship?"

"Yes."

"Does your daughter look forward to the contacts with her mother which you described," August referred to her notes, "having dinner together at your mother's, watching riding lessons, and regular phone calls?"

"Of course."

"Would you say your daughter is attached to your wife?"

"Yes."

"Mr. Grant, before you asked your wife to leave your home and before you took Livie to live with your mother, during that time when, as far as you knew, your marriage was happy, who made decisions about your daughter's schooling and after-school activities?"

"I would say it was fifty-fifty."

"So you made all the decisions together, or Mrs. Grant made half and you made half?"

Will squirmed in his chair. "Since she was home most of the time and I was working, Bennie made most of the decisions and kept me informed. If there was a big decision, she might ask my advice."

"From appearances, Mrs. Grant made good decisions, since your daughter is bright, healthy, and successful in school, isn't that so?"

"Of course."

"You referred to…" August flipped the pages of the yellow tablet. "normal disagreements you and your wife had from time to time."

Will repositioned himself again in the witness chair. "Yes, as any married couple will have."

"You mentioned specifically an example of such a disagreement—Mrs. Grant's desire to become active in the New Canaan amateur theater group. When you and Mrs. Grant married, she was attending Barnard College, majoring in stage directing. Is that correct, Mr. Grant?"

"Yes."

"Please describe the incident when you had a disagreement about her becoming involved in the New Canaan theater group."

Will looked at his attorney. Bell nodded.

"I came home from work one Friday evening, after a long week. Livie was probably about four years old at the time. The maid was just feeding her dinner. Normally, Bennie would have fed Livie, and she would have been cleaned up and in bed by the time I got home. I was concerned my daughter would not sleep well, eating so late. Bennie came in a few minutes later, all flushed and excited, and said she was at a Town Players audition, and they asked her to join."

"And what was your response?"

"I told her honestly I was against it. Those kinds of groups suck up your time, demanding more and more from you, and I didn't think her outside involvement would be good for Livie."

"Did she accede to your wishes?"

"I thought she had. We didn't speak of it again. The next Friday night I came home and was surprised to find the maid with Livie again. I ate dinner alone, and Bennie still hadn't come home, so I took Livie to my mother's, and we stayed for the weekend."

"Did you leave word with the maid or a note for Mrs. Grant as to where you had gone with your daughter?"

"No, but of course, she knew. She called and spoke with my mother, and Livie and I came home on Sunday. After consulting with my mother, I decided if the theater group meant so much to Bennie, we could work out a plan, and I told her so."

"What was her reaction?"

"Surprisingly, she had very little reaction, other than to say she would be joining the theater group."

"Mr. Grant, you appear to spend quite a bit of time being surprised by your wife's reactions."

Mr. Bell stood abruptly. "Objection, Your Honor!"

"Miss Mapes, a little less sarcasm, please."

"Sorry, Your Honor. Mr. Grant, do you drink alcoholic beverages?"

"Yes."

"Do you drink alcohol every day?"

"I suppose I do. I don't keep track of my consumption in detail. I'm a businessman, and discussing business over lunch is customary. Lunch usually involves a drink or two."

"During a normal business lunch, you would have one or two drinks?"

"Yes."

"In the evening, do you have alcohol before dinner?"

"Yes."

"How many drinks?"

"Usually two."

"Wine with dinner?"

"It depends. Sometimes we open a bottle of wine."

"Anything after dinner?"

"Maybe a brandy."

"So, Mr. Grant, would you describe yourself as a heavy drinker, four drinks a day, plus wine and brandy?"

"I would say I drink a normal amount for a man in my business."

August flipped through the pages of her yellow tablet again. "Mr. Grant, do you recall a conversation last Christmas Eve between you and Mrs. Grant in the residence hall at the girls' boarding school, her workplace?"

"Yes."

"How did you happen to be meeting with Mrs. Grant on Christmas Eve at the school?"

"I was at a party at the country club. The school is on the way from the club to my mother's, and I wanted to talk to Bennie about Livie. I called her and arranged to stop by."

"Did Mrs. Grant object to your stopping by at her place of work?"

"Yes, but I assured her I would be quick. I had a proposal for her. I knew most of the girls had gone home for the holidays."

"You mentioned you had been to a party. Had you been drinking at the party?"

"Yes."

"How many drinks would you say you had consumed?"

"In the space of the whole evening, maybe three or four."

"Did you also have a flask with you when you stopped by Mrs. Grant's school?"

"I don't remember for sure. I could have. I own a flask."

Mr. Bell rose again. "Your Honor, must we sit through another detailed inventory of Mr. Grant's alcohol consumption? I believe he has answered enough of these questions."

Judge stone nodded. "Move on to your point, Miss Mapes."

"What sort of proposal did you make to Mrs. Grant?"

"I said we should put the divorce on hold for six months and try to put our family back together, for Livie's sake."

"So even though you were aware Mrs. Grant had carried on an affair with her friend, you felt trying to reconcile your marriage was in your daughter's best interest."

"Yes."

"And what did you offer in consideration of Mrs. Grant's being willing to put the divorce off for six months?"

"That if she was still set on breaking up our family at the end of that time, I would consider joint custody."

"And if she wasn't willing to put the divorce off?"

"That I would immediately ask for full custody."

"And did Mrs. Grant agree with the postponement?"

"Yes."

"Yet here we are six months later and you're petitioning for full custody."

"My wife did not live up to the assurances she gave me."

"What assurances?"

"That the business with Alice Gifford was over. She flew all the way out to California to see her. She didn't give our reconciliation a real chance."

"Mr. Grant, on the Friday you arrived home from work and Mrs. Grant was at the theater group, you had dinner alone before taking Livie to your mother's. Would you say you had consumed about your normal amount of alcoholic drinks that day?"

"Probably."

"And you drove your daughter to your mother's house?"

"Yes, but I can assure you I was perfectly safe to drive."

"Thank you, Mr. Grant. No more questions, Your Honor."

August Mapes took her seat next to Bennie. The double doors in the rear of the courtroom opened. Bennie turned to see Olivia Grant and another woman enter, walk to the front of the room, and sit in the spectators' row behind Mr. Bell and Will. The woman with Olivia was Ina, the country club receptionist. Bennie felt the blood drain from her face.

Bennie's audible intake of breath caught August's attention.

"What is it?" August whispered, turning her head to follow Bennie's gaze. "Who is it?"

"It's Will's mother and someone else I need to tell you about. Can you get the judge to stop so we can talk?"

Judge Stone looked at his watch and toward Will's attorney. "Do you have redirect Mr. Bell?"

"Yes, Your Honor." Bell began to rise from his chair.

August stood up so quickly her chair made an urgent scraping sound.

"Your Honor, may we have a short recess before Mr. Bell begins?"

The judge nodded. "All right, fifteen minutes, and please be back promptly, everyone."

Attorneys in identical three-piece suits, carrying identical briefcases, crowded the cavernous marble hallway outside the courtroom. Their clients, looking as miserable as Bennie felt, leaned against the walls or milled about aimlessly. August found a vacant bench around the corner from their courtroom.

"Go ahead, Bennie. We have only a few minutes."

"The woman who came in with Will's mother is the receptionist at our country club. She checks everyone in at the front door and keeps a log of all the visitors and which club member is hosting him or her."

"Go on." August's voice was calm and even, but Bennie could sense her alert anticipation of bad news.

"This is complicated, and I know we don't have much time. That first day we met in your office, I mentioned a woman I'm interested in. We've kept each other at arm's length lately, until this custody battle is resolved, but Will could certainly use Laura against me if he found out about her."

August checked her watch. "We don't dare be late. What does this have to do with the receptionist?"

"Laura and I went to the country club a few weeks ago. She went as my guest. Olivia was at the club that day too, and she may have picked up on something between Laura and me. At least Laura thinks she might have. Also, Laura and I were together for a few days in California and Oregon, just before Will filed the divorce petition."

"Do they have any proof of something more than friendship between you?"

Bennie shook her head. "I don't think so, but why would Ina be here in court with Olivia?"

"It may just be a tactic. She isn't on Bell's witness list, and Judge Stone isn't likely to overlook the omission and let her testify. I hope we scored some points about Will's controlling nature and about his drinking. Bell's going to try and rehabilitate him during the redirect. We'll just have to see what happens. We have to go back." She stood and straightened her suit jacket.

After reminding Bennie and Will they were still under oath, Judge Stone instructed Mr. Bell to proceed.

"Mr. Grant, have you ever received a citation for driving under the influence of alcohol?"

"No."

"Have you been stopped for suspicion of driving under the influence?"

"No."

"Thank you. After Mrs. Grant began her involvement with Town Players of New Canaan, until your separation in July, did you attend various events and performances to support her?"

"Yes. Bennie was very successful, and I was proud of her."

"Thank you, Mr. Grant, that's all. Your Honor, we call Mrs. Olivia Grant."

Will stepped down and Olivia walked forward, nodding to the judge as she took the stand and raised her hand to be sworn in by the clerk.

"State your full name and address"

"Olivia Winslow Grant. 677 South Avenue, New Canaan, Connecticut."

Bennie sat on the edge of her seat, trying to steel herself for whatever was to come next.

"Mrs. Grant, since July last year, your son and his daughter have lived with you full time, is that correct?"

"Yes."

"Do you work outside the home, Mrs. Grant?"

Olivia smiled. "No."

"And so your days are devoted to making a home for your son and his daughter, and to your granddaughter's welfare."

"I have civic activities in the community and my own friends, of course, but most of these times are when Livie is in school."

"Would you say your son is a good father?"

Olivia beamed at Will. "He's very devoted to Livie. He has cut back on his work hours to spend as much time as possible with her. He's home for dinner almost every night with Livie and me."

"Have you ever known Mr. Grant to abuse alcohol?"

"No."

"Since July, when Mr. Grant and Livie came to live with you, has Livie spent time with her mother?"

"Bennie has always been welcome in my home. For a few months after she and Will separated, she came often for dinner with Will and Livie, and for a time I believe she was coming to watch Livie's riding lessons."

"Mrs. Grant, on how many occasions would you say Livie's mother has seen her in the last six months?"

"I believe her contact with Livie has been only by phone."

"Thank you, Mrs. Grant. No further questions, Your Honor."

"Miss Mapes?"

August rose. "Mrs. Grant, when your son and daughter-in-law were living together, did he sometimes ask your advice about his relationship with his wife?"

"Yes. When he was confused about how to make Bennie happy, he sometimes wanted my point-of-view."

"And since they separated, and your son brought Livie to live with you, does he continue to ask your advice about his relationship?"

"Yes."

'Were you aware that your son gave his wife an ultimatum about Livie six months ago?"

"Objection, Your Honor. Miss Mapes' characterization puts the witness in a bind. Any answer she gives acknowledges the loaded word 'ultimatum.'"

"Your Honor, I'll rephrase the question. Mrs. Grant, did you know that at Christmas, your son demanded his wife agree to a postponement of their divorce, and that he threatened to seek full custody of their daughter if she rejected the demand?"

"Yes."

Bennie saw the familiar thin line of Olivia's lips signaling her anger.

"Did Mr. Grant consult with you before presenting his wife with this demand?"

"Yes."

"What was Mr. Grant's purpose in presenting this demand?"

"He wanted to encourage Bennie to keep their marriage together for Livie's sake."

"What was your response when your son asked you for advice about his plan to coerce Mrs. Grant into putting off the divorce?"

"Objection, Your Honor. Her choice of words again."

Judge Stone pointed at August. "Miss Mapes, I'll tell you once more. Be careful."

August paused. "Mrs. Grant, what was your response when your son asked for advice about his plan to control his wife's going forward with the divorce by exploiting her fear of losing her daughter?"

Mr. Bell rose from his chair. "Your Honor."

Olivia Grant ignored her son's attorney and locked eyes with August. "I agreed with his plan. My son wants what's best for his daughter."

"Thank you, Mrs. Grant. No more questions, Your Honor."

"Any redirect, Mr. Bell?"

"No, Your Honor. We ask the Court to find that Mr. and Mrs. Grant's marriage should be terminated under the terms to which they both agree, and that Mr. Grant, with the assistance of his mother, Mrs. Olivia Grant, should have sole physical custody of the child, Olivia Elizabeth Grant. We rest our case."

"Miss Mapes, your turn. Off you go."

August stood at the podium.

"Your Honor, I call Mrs. Bennie Grant."

Bennie took the witness stand and stated her name and address. Seen this close, Judge Stone's stern demeaner softened a little. Up close he didn't seem quite so judgmental. He had a mass of silver hair and untamed eyebrows that partially hooded his alert gaze. The courtroom was so quiet Bennie could hear the beating of her own heart, and every face was turned toward her. Bennie focused her attention on August as she had been coached.

"Mrs. Grant, about a year ago, you told your husband that you wanted a divorce. Is that true?"

"Yes. I was terribly unhappy, and I thought Will felt the same, and Livie began noticing an unloving tension between us. The look on her face at those times broke my heart."

"Was this a spur-of-the-moment decision, your asking for the divorce?"

"No, I came to realize early in our marriage, before Livie was born, that we had made a mistake. We were just two mismatched people. I was very young when we married, and I had naive expectations of what our life would be like. I found my husband could be very controlling."

"What was Mr. Grant's reaction that night to your asking for a divorce?"

"He became extremely upset and kept demanding an explanation, beyond my unhappiness, for why I wanted a divorce."

"Mr. Grant has testified that you came home from a party, and that he had been drinking. Was he abusive or threatening during that conversation?"

"Not at first, but he kept badgering me to give him a 'good reason.' Finally, he asked if my unhappiness had anything to do with Alice Gifford, and I told him the truth, that we had become involved a year before and that it lasted only three months and that it had been over since then and that Alice was not the reason I wanted a divorce."

"What happened next?"

"He ordered me to leave. He said he couldn't be responsible for what he might do if I didn't leave. I packed a bag, called a taxi, and went to the Inn in the village. Olivia, Will's mother, let me speak with Livie on the phone the next day, but asked that I not try to see her. Over the next few weeks Will seemed to be coming to terms with the situation. He began bringing Livie to the Inn for dinner, the three of us. On one of those occasions, he proposed we start meeting with his attorney, Mr. Bell, to do what he called pre-divorce planning. I got a position teaching drama at

Mary Bradford School, and I lived in the senior residence hall as a counselor. Livie spent some weekends with me at the school."

"Were you represented by an attorney during the pre-divorce planning?"

"No. Mr. Bell was supposed to help us work things out without the situation becoming adversarial."

"As Judge Stone pointed out at the beginning," August said, "we are now in an adversarial situation. What happened to change things?"

"Will said he wanted to put our marriage back together. When we began to talk about custody of Livie, he balked. At Christmas, he came to my school and insisted we postpone the divorce. He threatened that if I didn't agree, he would fight me in court for full custody, and that's what he's doing."

"And you agreed?"

"I didn't feel I had a choice."

"And during this time, where has Livie been living?"

"At her grandmother's with Will."

"Do you and Mr. Grant consult on decisions involving Livie, such as her schooling and her outside activities?"

"No, Mr. Grant makes the decisions. He may consult with his mother."

Mr. Bell rose to his feet. "Objection, Your Honor. The witness is making guesses rather than stating facts."

"Sustained. Answer the question based on your direct knowledge, Mrs. Grant."

"Let's talk about a specific example, Mrs. Grant. Your eight-year-old daughter is taking jumping lessons on the pony her father gave her for Christmas, correct?"

"Yes."

"Did Mr. Grant consult you before buying her the pony, or before starting her on jumping lessons?"

"No."

"Whom did Mr. Grant consult before taking these steps?"

"He told me that he talked to a friend of his at the country club and to his mother."

"Did you object to your eight-year-old daughter taking jumping lessons?"

"I did. I was afraid she was too young and inexperienced with the pony, but he had already hired the jumping teacher and had told Livie. I didn't want to disappoint her."

"Mrs. Grant, on July fourth, when you first asked Mr. Grant for a divorce, you testified that he told you to leave and that…" August checked her yellow tablet, "he couldn't be responsible for what he might do if you didn't leave. Were you afraid for your physical safety?"

Will had been staring out the window when August asked the question. His attention snapped back to Bennie.

"I knew he had been drinking, and he was very angry."

"And when Mr. Grant came to your school on Christmas Eve, over your objection, did you have cause to feel afraid of him?"

"Again, he had been drinking, and he was very insistent on getting his way."

"Did you feel afraid he might physically harm you?"

"Yes."

Will whispered to his attorney who nodded and put a hand on his arm.

"Mrs. Grant, you are not asking for spousal support from Mr. Grant. Are you capable of providing a safe and loving home for your daughter?"

"Yes, I have a job and other financial resources from my grandmother's estate and I have a two-bedroom apartment so that she can have her own room."

"What about her school and her outside activities like her riding lessons?"

"I would want her to stay in her school and to keep on with her lessons. We could be together on weekends and during her summer vacations. I want to be able to visit with her in New Canaan also."

"Do you want to keep her away from her father and her grandmother?"

"No. My grandmother raised me after my mother passed away. My father lives in Portland, Oregon, but he traveled to New York often as I was growing up. These were wonderful relationships, and I would never deprive Livie of that."

"Mrs. Grant, did you recently travel to the West Coast?"

"Yes."

"What was the purpose of the trip?"

"The last six months have been very stressful. When the school term was over I went to visit for a few days with my friend in San Francisco and with my father in Portland. I was seeking their support and advice."

"Where did you stay in San Francisco?"

"At the Mark Hopkins Hotel."

"Mrs. Grant, is your romantic affair with Alice Gifford over?"

"Yes."

August gathered her papers. "Thank you, Mrs. Grant."

The judge looked at Will's attorney. "Cross examination, Mr. Bell?"

"Just a few questions, Your Honor. Mrs. Grant, when you flew to San Francisco, did you inform your husband of your whereabouts?"

"I left him my father's address and phone number."

"You didn't mention you were going directly to San Francisco, and that you would be seeing Alice Gifford?"

"No, I was concerned that he and his mother would misinterpret my motives for visiting Alice."

"So you were hiding your whereabouts from your husband and your daughter."

"I spoke with Livie every day."

"Did you make any attempt to speak with Mr. Grant during your visit with Alice Gifford in San Francisco?"

"No."

"Has your husband ever struck you, Mrs. Grant?"

"No."

"That's all, Your Honor."

"Redirect, Miss Mapes?"

"No, Your Honor."

Bennie looked at the judge.

"You're done, Mrs. Grant. You may step down."

As soon as Bennie took her seat beside August, she wrote a note on the yellow legal tablet. *They're not calling Ina?*

As we thought, a ploy, August wrote back.

"Do you have any final words, Miss Mapes?"

"Mr. Grant and his mother are asking the court to find that keeping a little girl away from her mother is the best thing for the child's welfare. No matter how well-intentioned they are, Livie needs the attention and influence of her mother. Having consistent contact with two loving parents, along with her grandmother, is the best outcome for Livie. Even though, regrettably, the parents can no longer live together, Mrs. Grant believes that they can all work together to give their best to their daughter. We request that Mrs. Grant have shared custody and that she be able to have her daughter on alternating weekends and holidays and during the summer months when Livie is out of school."

Judge Stone looked over his reading glasses at Bennie and Will. "Mr. Grant, Mrs. Grant, I've listened to your testimony and heard the arguments of your counsel as to the facts about the custody of your daughter. We'll break until one-thirty, at which time I will render my decision."

Chapter Thirty-One

Back in the courtroom after the break, they waited for the judge to return. Will and Mr. Bell were turned around in their chairs, carrying on a whispered conversation with Olivia. Ina had left. Bennie smiled to herself as she imagined an uncomfortable scene in which Olivia tried to explain to the receptionist exactly why she was needed in court.

"All rise," the bailiff ordered.

Judge Stone took his seat. "Mr. and Mrs. Grant, my concern in reviewing this custody petition is the welfare of your child. In cases such as this, it would be customary to assume that the mother is the natural custodian of a female child of this age."

With a surge of hope, Bennie sat up straighter in her chair.

"However, Mrs. Grant, by your own admission, you have engaged in unnatural, inappropriate, and illegal behavior. My job here is not to punish you for that, but to consider how your behavior might bear on what is in your child's best interests."

The judge turned to Will. "Mr. Grant, you are a successful businessman and a responsible provider for your family. You clearly are proud of your daughter and devoted to her. Having the support of your mother, your child's grandmother, is also an important factor. However, you have acknowledged that your daughter has a deep bond with her mother. We must assume that severing that bond would harm the child.

"One additional step that I might take is to talk with Olivia Elizabeth directly. You say she is bright. She could be old enough to express a choice, if she were asked."

"No!" Bennie shouted, rising from her chair. "No, I won't agree to that. You told us how harmful all this could be for her. I won't put her through it."

"Mrs. Grant, I must insist you control yourself."

August stood, put her arm around Bennie's shoulder and encouraged her back into her seat.

The judge gathered the papers in front of him. "In the absence of any more facts, I'm ready to rule." He paused and looked from Mr. Bell to August. "I am granting the father's petition for sole physical custody, with the provision that the mother be given unlimited in-person visits with the child in the company of either Mr. Grant, or his mother."

The judge turned his penetrating gaze to Will. "Mr. Grant, I'm ordering that you make all efforts to facilitate Olivia Elizabeth's spending time with her mother."

The judge turned to Bennie. "Mrs. Grant, it's my understanding that psychotherapy can be effective in certain cases of disorders like yours. You can come back to this court for reconsideration if your situation changes. That's all." He handed the stack of papers to the clerk.

Bennie sank in her chair and covered her face with her hands.

August searched in her bag for a tissue. "Hold yourself together until they leave."

Bennie heard the screech of the hinge on the waist-high gate separating the principals' tables from the viewing area.

"They're gone." August handed Bennie the tissue. "I'm so sorry."

"I know."

"We can appeal. The judge left the door open a crack. It would mean you'd have to let Livie talk to him. It wouldn't necessarily be in open court."

Bennie shook her head. "I won't be the reason she has to go through that. Can you imagine him asking my child to choose between her father and me? Thank you, August. I know you did everything you could. Let's get out of here."

In front of the courthouse, she and August watched as Will helped his mother into the back seat of their car. He turned toward Bennie and raised his hand in a tentative gesture that seemed to Bennie to be a mixture of regret and farewell.

In spite of the heat and humidity making the air shimmer off the sidewalk, Bennie decided to walk uptown rather than share a taxi with August. In a mental fog, she turned north and let the swirl of foot traffic carry her mindlessly past shops and cafes, dry cleaners and delis through the Village. After several blocks, she walked beside the new red brick, multi-storied apartment buildings of Stuyvesant Town, built for men returning home and women returning to kitchens after the war. Bennie thought the buildings looked more like a middle-class prison than a sanctuary for families.

She crossed west on a quiet residential street lined with brownstones. A horse-drawn ragpicker's cart clopped past her, the sleepy horse lazily swatting flies with her tail. Farther on, she passed a candy store where three little girls only slightly older than Livie burst from the door onto the sidewalk, giggling and clutching their prizes of penny candy.

At the corner of Broadway and 44th in Times Square, the realization of the morning's events overwhelmed her. She ducked into a drugstore where a waitress in a starched pink uniform, apron, and cap took her order for coffee. Bennie sat staring across Broadway at a Camel cigarette billboard with a giant picture of a man's head blowing a five-foot smoke ring every few seconds.

Phone booths lined the drugstore's wall beside the cash register. She fished in her purse for phone change and pulled out the psychiatrist's business card. She stared at the card, tore it in half, and dropped it in the ashtray. She went to a phone booth and dialed Laura's number.

"Bennie, where are you? What happened in court?"

She let out a sob when she heard Laura's voice. "I lost utterly."

"You sound terrible. Tell me where you are. Wait there. I'll come to you."

While Bennie waited, she counted the smoke rings coming from the billboard and watched the drugstore fill with office workers stopping in from the surrounding businesses for the "Sundries and Sundaes" the sign in the front window advertised. Across the crowded store, Laura appeared at the door and stood a moment looking over the customers until she located Bennie and rushed over to sit at the small table across from her.

"What do you mean, you lost utterly?"

"The judge awarded sole custody to Will. I can have visits with Livie, but they must be supervised by Will or his mother, which is almost worse than not seeing her at all. Can you imagine Livie beginning to treat me as some kind of distant relation? I'd rather wait until she can make her own decisions about seeing me."

"Can't you appeal it?"

"I'd have to let them involve Livie. I won't put her through that."

"You may change your mind."

Bennie shook her head.

Laura lit a cigarette and picked up the business card from the ashtray to read it.

She arched her eyebrows. "Yours?"

"In court, the judge recommended psychotherapy for my disorder."

"Oh, my darling. How perfectly horrible this has all been for you." She took Bennie's hand. "This may not be the time, but, well, these last few weeks, I've been looking at apartments on my own, away from Charles. I was thinking that maybe you'd want to live with me. You wouldn't have to worry about anything. You can work as many hours as you need to. We'll have a housekeeper, and a cook if you want. We can go to New Canaan to see Livie as often as you like."

"Stop." Bennie put her hand over Laura's. "You're moving away from Charles? What's behind this?"

"I want you, Bennie, and I want to help you with your daughter, however I can. I want a life with you. I want to live with you. You've given me the courage to recognize it."

"Yes." Bennie's answer was fast and unequivocal.

"Yes?"

"Yes."

"Well, all right. All right. I'm delighted. Let's go find our apartment."

Chapter Thirty-Two

Bennie sat on the couch in front of the fire, scratching the special spot under Scout's chin where the white hairs were starting to pepper his shiny black coat. A steady, rhythmic thwacking sound, amplified by the still, cold air and thick blanket of snow, drifted from the property next door. The neighbor was chopping firewood across the stream that formed a boundary line between their properties.

She looked across the room at Laura bending over a drafting table in front of the east-facing window. Her dark hair, laced with grey, fell forward over her face. As with every time Bennie glimpsed Laura across a room, she felt a little burst of emotion in her solar plexus. Laura had grown even more beautiful over the ten years they had been together. "Isn't Mr. Fletcher's chopping bothering your concentration?"

Laura didn't look up. "No. An honest man doing honest work. It's kind of soothing really."

Scout whined his insistence that she keep scratching. She chuckled when he let out a moan.

"What?"

"I was just laughing at Scout's moan. Have you noticed how much grey hair he's getting? It seems like yesterday he was a puppy. When we first got together. He's an old man now."

"That was in 1951."

"I'm surprised you remember the date."

Laura looked up, then back at her drawing. "Don't be silly. Of course I do."

"I'll bet you don't remember the first night we met."

"I remember it very well. You came to my house in New Canaan for dinner."

"That was the second time. I was already madly in love with you when I came to dinner."

"You tell me then." Laura crossed her arms and leaned back in her chair. "When was the first time we met?"

"The first time I ever saw you was at the annual Revel at Mary Bradford School and at the reception afterward. It was just before Christmas in 1950. You were standing in the center of a group of stuffy old men, other board members of the school, and they were hanging on your every word. You wore a Chanel suit, and you had this mannerism, that you still have by the way, of holding the jacket back with your hand at the waist. You were magnificent."

"I remember the Revel and the reception because it was my first function as a board member, but you're right. I don't remember our meeting that night."

"No reason you'd remember the headmistress introducing us. I was just a teacher. Little did you know that I began that night hatching my diabolical plan to ensnare you."

"Lucky me."

Bennie pushed up from the couch, padded to the kitchen in her socked feet for the coffeepot, and went over to freshen Laura's cup. She looked over Laura's shoulder at the drawing on the drafting table. "Is that the re-do of the Pierre? Are you working even on holiday? I thought you had a long time to get it ready."

"It re-opens in June, and the new owners are expecting spectacular results before then. I'm struggling to come up with a starting concept. Hope I haven't bitten off more than I can chew with this one. I woke up this morning with some ideas, and I want to get them on paper while they're fresh."

"You make me feel guilty. If I'm going to take on the Ibsen revival, which I'm seriously considering, I should be thinking about casting. *Hedda Gabler* will be a big stretch for me. Not my usual frothy musical. If I had a great Hedda lined up, it would make me feel a lot more confident."

"Who are you thinking of?"

"Well, that's the rub. I don't have any good ideas. I was thinking of asking Miss LeG's advice. I've always envied her talent for casting just the right actors."

"It's funny to me that after all these years and all your success in the theater, you still call Eva LeGallienne, Miss LeG."

"It's a term of affection as well as one of respect. She's my mentor, and she gave me my first break as an assistant director, you remember."

"I know. Maybe I'm still a little jealous of her."

Bennie stroked her chin. "Hmm. She is a very attractive woman, all right."

Laura dropped her pencil, encircled Bennie's waist, and pulled her close. "I knew it! I knew she had more on her mind than mentoring." She buried her nose in Bennie's stomach. "You smell good. Let's go back to bed." She pulled Bennie onto her lap.

"Careful, you'll make me spill. Your offer is very tempting, now that I have your attention, but no. I'm distracting you. Do you think we could dig the car out later and go to the Inn for dinner?"

"Cabin fever?"

"No."

"Do you wish we'd stayed in town for Christmas? We could have. I suspect you're missing Livie. This is our first Christmas away from your daughter in all these years."

"She's totally consumed with being a freshman at Barnard and her friends there. I suspect her father and grandmother won't see much of her in Connecticut this Christmas, either."

"So you don't have cabin fever, and you're not pining for Livie. Are you missing all those chic pre-Christmas cocktail parties in New York?"

Bennie shook her head. "Cocktail parties aren't as chic as they used to be. I'm not wishing to be in New York at all. I love it here. I want to go out for dinner tonight because I like being out with you and seeing the admiring looks you get. It makes me proud. I read somewhere that it's good for couples to see each other through outside eyes once in a while. Makes us appreciate what we have."

Laura pulled her close and nuzzled her neck. "Of course we can go out, but if you weren't so clueless about how gorgeous you are, you'd notice that those admiring looks are for you. Anyway, call the Inn and get a table in the middle of the room so as many people as possible can admire both of us." She chuckled at her own joke, a sound that came from deep in her throat. Bennie always found it sexy beyond description.

Bennie jabbed a finger in her ribs. "Very funny." She stood and turned Laura's chair back to the desk. "Get to work, and Scout and I will call for a dinner reservation. Then maybe I'll try and commune with Mr. Ibsen about the perfect Hedda. Or, maybe we'll just sit by the fire and listen to the snow fall."

Laura had already gone back to her sketching. "Snow falling doesn't make a sound. It's the epitome of silence."

"I was making a joke. How can someone as creative as you be so literal sometimes?"

Laura shrugged. "Part of my mysterious charm."

Bennie had her hand on the telephone when it rang. She jumped and jerked her hand away. "Who in the world?" She picked up on the second ring. "Hello?"

"Mother, it's me."

"Livie, is everything all right?"

Laura looked up.

"Yes, yes. I'm at school, so don't be surprised to hear me dropping coins in the pay phone. Everything's fine. Most people are gone for the holidays."

"Are you alone there in the dorm?"

"Elaine was here until an hour ago. She's going home to Chicago."

"I thought she planned to go with you to Connecticut to your grandmother's?"

"That's what I'm calling about. Could I come to Vermont? I know it's short notice."

"You'd like to come to Vermont?" Bennie looked at Laura and mouthed, "Okay?"

Laura nodded.

"Of course, you can come to Vermont, baby, but are your father and grandmother on board with this?"

"I haven't told them yet. I'm planning to, but I wanted to make sure it was okay with you first. I know you'll say they'll be disappointed, and that it's rude, but I've already told Father not to expect to see me much over the holidays. I checked the plane schedules, and I can be there tomorrow afternoon, if you and Laura can pick me up at the airport in Burlington."

Bennie pictured her ex-mother-in-law sitting by a roaring fire in her perfect library in her perfect neo-Tutor mansion. The whole house would be lavishly decorated, inside and out, with a thousand green and red lights. She'd be counting on Livie to flip the switch at midnight on Christmas eve, as she did every year since she was a little girl.

"They will be disappointed." Bennie felt ambivalent. She'd love seeing her daughter, but she knew Olivia would be fit to be tied, and that she would blame Bennie. She swallowed her hesitation. "Of course you can come."

Livie gave the details of her flight from New York to Burlington. "And, Mother, do you think you and I could go ice skating, just the two of us? Would Laura feel left out?"

"I don't think so. She's working on the interior design for her next big project. She'll probably welcome the time to focus on that. We can ask her when you get here."

The operator broke in demanding another infusion of coins to continue the call. "Bye, Mother. I'll see you tomorrow afternoon."

Bennie hung up the phone and sat with her hand resting on the receiver. "What do you suppose that's all about?"

"What did she say?"

"Just that she wants to come, and that she wants to go ice skating, just the two of us." Bennie smiled. "She was concerned you might feel left out. I suspect you'd rather be horsewhipped than hike up that hill to the pond in the cold."

"You know me so well, my love. Leave me here by this nice, warm fire."

Bennie sipped her coffee and made a face because it had gotten cold. "Something's going on with her, and I hope it doesn't spoil our holiday."

"Maybe she just wants to be with you at Christmas."

"Maybe…but it didn't sound that way."

Laura stood up and began to put her papers away. "Let's go into the village now instead of waiting till dinner. We can have a nice lunch and a quiet night at home. She pulled Bennie close. "You can give me an early present in front of the fire under the Christmas tree."

"We don't have a Christmas tree."

"Now who's being literal?"

Chapter Thirty-Three

Laura steered the Range Rover next to the curb at the Burlington airport.

"How do you do that so perfectly every time? I'll never learn to drive as well as you." Bennie caressed Laura's thigh. "I've always found your driving very sexy."

Laura patted Bennie's hand. "You're sweet, and a little silly. I'll find a parking spot and meet you and Livie at baggage claim."

Bennie swung the passenger door open and let in a recorded female voice that managed to sound authoritative and pleasant at the same time. "The white zone is for the loading and unloading of passengers only."

The baggage area buzzed with excited conversation. The crowd around the lone baggage carousel were mostly young people coming to Stowe for holiday skiing. A loud squawk signaled luggage arriving from the New York flight. Duffle bags, ski boot cases, and skis carriers began piling onto the baggage merry-go-round. Bennie stood back from the crowd on tiptoe, searching for Livie's blond ponytail. A thin girl with short blonde curls caught her eye. *Could it be Livie? She seemed taller, and had she cut her hair?* A young man next to her grabbed the girl's bag off the carousel and said something that made the girl laugh. Bennie recognized the sound.

"Livie!" Bennie rushed over and hugged her daughter. "I hardly knew you. You can't be taller than in September. Are you?"

"I don't think so. Mother, this is Tim. We sat next to each other on the plane. He's at Columbia." Livie took her bag. "Well, good skiing."

He was reluctant to say goodbye. "I didn't get your number. What dorm are you in?"

"Hewitt."

"Okay. Well. See you on campus, maybe."

"Yes, maybe."

They headed toward the exit, and Bennie put her arm around her daughter's shoulders. "He was cute."

Livie shrugged.

"Anyway, we're so glad you decided to come. You've cut your hair. It's darling."

"It's a lot more practical. It takes hardly any time now. Where's Laura?"

"Parking the car. She must have had trouble finding a spot. We'll wait for her outside."

Laura jaywalked toward them through a line of slow-moving cars and trucks, all with luggage and skis piled on top. She embraced Livie and held her at arm's length. "Most people gain weight from dorm food, but I think you've lost some."

"I think she's taller. Look, she's almost your height."

"And your hair's darling."

"My words, exactly."

Livie pulled on a lemon-yellow and red knit cap with a red pom-pom on top. "You're both making me feel self-conscious. I'm exactly the same dimensions as before, except with shorter hair."

Laura took her bag. "The car's over this way. I found a close spot."

Bennie looped her arm through Livie's. "That's what took her so long. She was circling the lot looking for the perfect parking place. She always does that. Drives me crazy."

They crossed the slushy airport access lanes, dodging rooster tails of muddy water thrown up by the traffic. Bennie stowed Livie's duffle bag behind the back seat and encouraged her to take the shotgun position. "So I can feast my eyes on you without having to look backward, which makes me carsick."

Bennie peppered Livie with questions about her first semester at Barnard. Livie had been accepted by Stanford in Palo Alto, California, and it seemed sure that she'd choose the prestigious and highly competitive school, thousands of miles away. Bennie had been pleasantly surprised when Livie chose the women's liberal arts college in Manhattan instead.

"Are you glad you decided on Barnard?"

"I think so. I don't have anything to compare it with firsthand. I like that we don't have football and the rest of that ra-ra stuff. Living in Manhattan is fun, not in some college town in the middle of nowhere."

"I doubt Palo Alto, California, would enjoy being characterized as the middle of nowhere. Laura and I had a wonderful driving trip up the coast of California a few years ago." Laura gave her a smile in the rearview mirror.

"You know what I mean. Other college towns seem to be so insular. The Upper West Side of Manhattan is our college town. Another thing I like is that they encourage us to think for ourselves."

"Have you decided on a major yet?"

"No. I'm taking requirements so far. I like history though." Livie leaned her forehead against the side window glass. "World history, not just American history."

"What about your dorm? I lived in Hewitt too, you know. The place was ancient even then. You should see it, Laura. You'd be outraged. The plumbing was totally unreliable and the radiators made awful noises all night. Is the elevator still broken?"

"Yes, but freshmen live on the first floor."

"That's right. One more semester, then you move up a floor."

Livie didn't respond. She blew her breath on the window and wrote her initials in the haze.

Laura caught Bennie's eye in the rearview mirror and raised her brows. "Let's have some Christmas cheer." She clicked on the radio and found carols, but she kept fiddling with the dial. "I don't like these modern songs. Give me some good old-fashioned 'Jingle Bells' and 'Silent Night.'" She finally settled on a station that filled in the silence as they drove the rest of the way to Stowe.

At the city limits, Highway 100 became Main Street, busy with bundled-up locals weighed down with shopping bags. The ski crowd were lined up outside Jake's, the town's only diner. Lamp posts and leafless trees twinkled with red and green lights.

Laura turned off the radio and rolled down her window to let in the music of chimes from the First Presbyterian Church. "Now that's more like it." She looked over at Livie, with her forehead still pressed to the window. "Hey, you two. We can cut a Christmas tree in the woods, but we don't have any decorations."

Bennie leaned forward to brush Livie's cheek and tuck a blond curl under her knit cap. "Stop here at the general store. We'll get some construction paper and make our own. Come in with me, sweetie, and help me pick the right colors."

Laura waited for a car pulling out of a spot in front of the store. She grinned at Bennie. "Perfect spot."

Chapter Thirty-Four

Laura poured steaming hot chocolate into a thermos. She watched Livie bite her bottom lip in concentration as she spread peanut butter and grape jelly on slices of wheat bread. "You really are your grandmother's granddaughter. I suspect Olivia would take the same kind of care to make those sandwiches perfect."

Livie's cheeks colored. "I didn't know you were watching me. Yes, I can be a little compulsive sometimes. I like to think it's genetic. Something beyond my control."

They heard the rush of the shower in the next room. "Sounds like your mother is finally waking up. I think she may have had a little too much eggnog last night while we were decorating the tree." She looked over at the evergreen in the corner to the left of her desk. "Which looks very fine, if I do say so myself."

"That was so much fun. Do you think Mother will still want to go skating?"

"I'm sure she wouldn't miss it for the world."

Livie paused over the sandwiches, considering whether to cut off the crusts. Instead, she cut each sandwich into four perfect triangles. "Elaine teases me about being compulsive too. She says if you're too careful, you're so occupied with being careful that you're sure to miss what's right in front of you."

"Elaine plans to go to medical school, doesn't she? Surely doctors have to be careful types."

"She's not going to be that kind of doctor. She wants to specialize in public health and study whole populations of people and work on how poverty, famine, and war affect their health. Columbia has the best program in the country to study that."

Laura could picture serious, brilliant Elaine having this same conversation with Livie. She would be pacing and gesturing passionately as she described her future. Laura and Bennie speculated about Livie's and Elaine's relationship, whether they might be more than friends. They picked through Livie's letters and phone calls to Bennie for clues, but so far Livie hadn't volunteered any information. "She'll let us know when she's ready," they told each other.

"Bennie mentioned Elaine will be finishing Barnard early and starting medical school next semester, right?"

"She's not sure yet." Livie tore off plastic wrap and made neat PB and J packets. "Laura, you've mentioned you didn't go to college. Do you mind talking about it? Do you regret it?"

"I used to mind talking about it, when I was younger and had yet to accomplish anything worthwhile. I felt inadequate at times." Laura screwed the top on the thermos. "But I was lucky to find a career that was just the right fit. Sometimes I wonder if my life would have been different if I had gone to college, but then I think, how could it be any better?"

"Why didn't you go?"

"I had a job, on the bottom rung, just starting out, but making a steady salary. I thought about saving to enroll in NYU, but buying a car seemed more important. Mind you, it was a different time. The country was deep in the Great Depression. I was very lucky to have a good job."

"What about your parents? They wouldn't send you to college?"

"My father didn't believe in higher education for girls."

***

Scout bounded into the room. In his excitement, he pranced around on tiptoes, jumped up, and turned a complete circle in the air. Livie laughed and clapped. "Look at him! How does he do that?"

Bennie came in behind him toweling her hair dry. "We once went to a dinner party, and the host had a psychic for entertainment. She told us he thinks he can fly. What are you two talking so intently about?"

Livie glanced at Laura. "We're just waiting for you to get ready. You do still want to go, right?"

"I wouldn't miss it for the world."

Bennie and Livie sat on a bench in the mudroom to tie the laces of their skates together and slung them over their shoulders. Livie shrugged into the straps of the backpack with their sandwiches and hot chocolate. Laura buttoned the top button on Bennie's bright-red down jacket and knotted her wool scarf tighter around her neck. She pulled her in for a quick kiss on the cheek. "Have a good time, darling, and don't break anything." She zipped Livie's jacket higher. "Don't you either."

Bennie and Livie went down the back steps and struck out toward Scarlet Oak Pond. The trail rose gently at first and became steeper as they ascended. The snow on the pathway had been packed down by snowmobiles and earlier hikers. Livie took the lead and set a steady pace. It made Bennie smile that her daughter looked back over her shoulder often to make sure that Bennie could keep up. The trail leveled out and became broader.

Bennie put her arm around Livie's waist and pulled Livie's arm around hers. "Let's walk together. Look, we have each other's rhythm perfectly. Let's sing a marching song."

She started the first one that came to her mind, "The Halls of Montezuma." They marched along, singing at the tops of their lungs, the sound muffled by snow and heavy cold air. The huge oak tree for which the pond was named came into view. There were other skaters circling counterclockwise around the pond and four boys in the middle slapping a hockey puck back and forth. Someone had lit a fire in an old oil drum, encircled by stump seats. They sat on two of the stumps to lace up their skates and merged into the crowd of skaters.

Bennie ran out of steam before Livie. "I'm going to sit by the fire a while. Show me some tricks. I haven't seen you skate in years."

"I'm ready for a rest too. There's something I need to talk to you about."

They took seats on stumps next to each other and Bennie took Livie's hands in hers and chaffed them together to warm them up.

Livie blew out a breath that turned into an icy cloud in the frigid air. She gazed across the pond over the tops of the snow-covered pine trees and shook her head. "I'm just going to come out with it."

"All right."

"I'm not going back to school for next semester."

"Oh?" Bennie felt her stomach drop.

"It may seem that this is an impulsive decision, but it's not. I've thought everything through carefully." She turned to Bennie. "I know you'll say you're against it but just hear me out." She took a breath and sat up straighter. "Elaine is joining the Peace Corps and I'm going with her."

"Elaine's convinced you to join the Peace Corps with her?"

"No, she hasn't convinced me. In fact, she's not entirely for it, but it's not her decision. It's not anybody's but mine. I haven't told Father and Grandmother yet, and I know they'll try to talk me out of it."

Bennie fought down a selfish feeling of panic. She could imagine Will and Olivia getting this news. They wouldn't just talk. If that didn't work, they would bribe, cajole, and threaten, and Bennie would be expected to go along with their tactics.

Livie scooted toward the edge of her seat. "Mother, with what's going on in the world, Elaine and I want to do something real. We're going to Thailand."

"Thailand! Why Thailand?"

"Refugees are pouring in there from Vietnam. The country is asking for help from the United States. We aren't in the war yet, even though we are headed there. Elaine is going to be a health aide, and I'm going to be a teaching assistant."

"I thought you have to be a college graduate to volunteer for the Peace Corps." Bennie's mind was groping for practical arguments against what Livie wanted to do. Her internal reaction was viscerally emotional. Her little girl, going to a dangerous part of the world, halfway across the globe.

"It depends on the host country, and since Thailand's needs are so great because of the war, they're accepting people who have the willingness and an aptitude for languages. Mother, you've seen the pictures of children sprayed with napalm. Do you know what napalm is? It's burning gasoline that they make into a jelly so it sticks to the body longer. It's meant to instill terror."

Bennie shivered with revulsion.

Livie took Bennie's hands. "I need your help. Elaine's twenty-one, so she can sign up on her own. Since I'm only nineteen, I need a parent's approval. I need you to sign for me. You'll do it, won't you?"

Bennie watched a skater who she figured was about twelve years old. She was tall and thin and as graceful in her strides and spins as a colt. She looked over at the two of them with a beatific smile, sensing that Bennie was admiring her. Bennie wished Livie were twelve again. They hadn't always gotten along then, but in hindsight, their problems seemed small and manageable compared with this development.

"Won't you sign for me?" When Bennie didn't respond, Livie dropped her hands. "If you won't, I'll just go anyway, without the backing of the Peace Corps."

"Livie, honey, you're being unfair. You have to give me some time to absorb what you're thinking about. This is a big step, and dangerous. I have to wrap my head around what to do. You know I've worked very hard all these years to keep a civil relationship with your father and grandmother. They'll be terribly against this, and if I sign for you without your even talking with them, they'll use it against me."

Livie nodded. "I'm sorry. I'm putting you in a terrible position, but there's not much time. We have to leave in the middle of January. Elaine's in Chicago telling her parents right now." She began loosening the laces on her skates. "You're right though. I'll go to Connecticut and talk to them right away." She looked up. "But you're not saying you're against me going, right?"

"I guess I'm putting off saying that. What I'm feeling now is overwhelming dread of you being so far away beyond my power to protect you."

Livie knelt in the snow in front of Bennie and began unlacing her skates. "I'll settle for that answer right now."

They held hands and picked their way down the trail that had iced over since the climb up. Back home, they stamped the snow off their boots in the mudroom.

***

Laura met them with warm fluffy towels. "Here are my winter fairy princesses, back from the enchanted forest…" She stopped her teasing mid-sentence when she saw their faces. "What's the matter? What happened?"

Bennie hung her jacket on a peg. "Let's go into the living room by the fire."

Laura listened without comment as Livie told her the plan to join the Peace Corps with Elaine and go to Thailand. "Because I'm not twenty-one yet, I need a parent's signature."

"Let me guess. You're asking Bennie, not your father."

"I was, but I see now that it puts her in a terrible position. I'm going to fly back tomorrow to tell Father and Grandmother."

Bennie spoke up. "And I'm going to fly back with you."

Laura shook her head. "Nonsense. We'll all drive back together."

Chapter Thirty-Five

It was a five-hour drive from Stowe to New Canaan in good weather. They left at dawn, Laura and Bennie up front, Livie in the middle seat, and Scout sharing the back with their luggage.

It started snowing just outside the city limits, and two hours into the trip, grey clouds settled over the highway, bringing a heavy snowstorm. Laura sat slightly forward, concentrating on navigating the slippery road ahead. She glanced over at Bennie and gestured toward Livie napping in the back. "She's worn out."

"I'm not surprised. I heard her moving around in the living room all night. I don't think she slept."

"She has a difficult day ahead, facing her father and grandmother with this news."

Bennie nodded. The tires hummed steadily over the road. If the truth were known, she hadn't slept much either. If her mind had been easier, she would have nodded off here in the car. Instead, she replayed the last ten years since the custody trial as though they were on a continuous loop. She started with the custody hearing and Judge Stone's solemn warning that she might be harming her child by fighting for joint custody in open court. Her thoughts moved to the judge's awful verdict, sole physical custody of her child to Will. She would be allowed to see Livie only in the presence of her ex-husband or, even more terrible, her ex-mother-in-law.

Laura was stalwart during the next years. She and Bennie went to New Canaan every Sunday they could get away from their busy careers so that Bennie could have lunch in the village with Will and Livie. She never criticized when Bennie impulsively jumped on the train mid-week to stand across the street from Livie's school and watch her at recess. Bennie called Livie every morning before school, went to every equestrian event, and when Livie lost interest in horses and took up competitive diving, she attended every meet she could. Life was all about work and Livie, and Laura never complained.

They stopped only once for gas, sandwiches, and coffee, and to let Scout relieve himself. At the border between Massachusetts and Connecticut, the storm broke, the clouds parted, and the sun shone through. Laura blew out a breath. "Thank goodness. I take this as a very good sign, ladies."

Two hours later, they turned off the main road past New Canaan village onto the driveway of the Grant mansion. As they rounded the last bend, the three-story brick and stucco façade came into view.

Livie began gathering her things. "I'll get to light the tree again this year. That's something good, right?"

Laura pulled up next to the broad front steps. Livie opened the door and jumped out. "Just let me get my duffle bag. You don't have to come in."

"Are you sure, honey?"

"Yes."

***

The day after Christmas, Fifth Avenue was a hopeless snarl. Bennie craned her neck from the back seat of the taxi, and all she could see was an endless line of yellow. She checked her watch. "Pull over here, please."

She stepped out of the taxi and onto the curb. A frigid north wind made her eyes water, picking up the edge of her scarf and flapping it like a flag. She pulled her fur coat tighter and walked as fast as she could, swearing at her decision to wear high heels. She had intended to be early for her meeting with Will in the Palm Court, and now she'd be late. After four blocks, the red-carpeted front steps of the Plaza Hotel came into view. She slowed to catch her breath.

The doorman touched the bill of his cap and held the door for her, as she entered into the blessedly warm lobby of the hotel. Straight ahead, the Palm Court was bright with amber-colored sunlight filtering through the glass mosaic ceiling. Will was already seated at a secluded table between a marble column and a huge potted palm.

He stood to help her off with her coat and held her chair. "What would you like? A drink?"

"Just tea to thaw me out."

He signaled the waiter and ordered tea for her and his usual scotch on the rocks. "You look marvelous, as you always do."

"Thank you, Will. You look well too." Bennie meant the compliment. Will had aged well. His salt and pepper hair was more salt now, and he had grown a beard, which gave the illusion of squaring off his chin.

Bennie was surprised when he blushed a little. "I try and stay in shape." He raised his glass of scotch. "Haven't given this up though." He looked around. "The last time we were together, just the two of us, was in this very room. That didn't go so well, as I recall. It was before the divorce. I had hoped I could convince you to agree to Mother and me having sole custody of Livie without the need to go to court and air our dirty linen." He shook his head. "I hope you will let me apologize all these years later."

Apologize for what exactly? For fighting to keep Livie away from me or for assuming he could have just talked me into agreeing? She held her tongue. She needed to keep this discussion civil for Livie's sake.

He filled in the awkward silence by signaling the waiter for another scotch. "What's Laura up to these days?"

"Her firm is redecorating the Pierre. She's over there right now."

"Good for her. The word on the street is that the new owner is a Saudi who's made of money and sparing no expense."

Bennie set her teacup down harder than she intended, and the sound startled them both. "Can we get to the point, Will? We need to talk about Livie."

Will nodded.

"What did she tell you?"

"She sat Mother and me down after Christmas Eve dinner and laid out a case for leaving school for eighteen months and volunteering with the Peace Corps in Thailand. She had done all the research and had her facts together, and she's obviously very passionate about the cause. She said she needs a parent to sign."

"What did your mother say?"

"She didn't hear a word beyond Livie saying, 'I'm leaving school and joining the Peace Corps.' She pretended to listen, let Livie say her piece, then said, 'Your father and I will discuss it.'"

"She has no intention of going along, right?"

Will shook his head and drew out the word, "No."

"Did Livie tell you what she told me, that she will go to Thailand with or without our approval?"

"No. Do you think she would?"

"Unless we can change her mind."

"I'm not so sure we should try."

Bennie leaned forward. "What are you saying?"

Will signaled the waiter to freshen Bennie's tea. "Let me tell you a story we've never spoken about. When you and I met at that dance, you saw a privileged young man in a hand-tailored uniform with a desk job at the War Department in Washington. What you didn't know was that it was not what I wanted. The day after the Japanese bombed Pearl Harbor, like most other able-bodied men in the country, I packed my bags and enlisted in the Army.

"After basic training, I got orders for a desk job in DC. I put in transfer request after request, every week, but the reassignment never came through. Finally, to shut me up, my commanding officer told me that mine was considered a special file. Father had just died, and my mother called in favors from his friends in high places to keep me in the country and out of Europe or the Pacific.

"I was furious. I confronted her, and she broke down. It was the only time I've ever seen my mother cry. She said she simply couldn't live with the possibility of losing me so soon after losing Father. I left her sobbing and went back to Washington. We never spoke of it again."

Bennie tried to get a picture of the steely Olivia that she knew losing control as Will described.

"Livie is a wonderful person. I'm not sure if that's partly because of us, you, Mother, and me, or sometimes in spite of us. The only problem we've ever had with her was when she was fourteen, and she refused to wear a white gown and long white gloves and participate in the cotillion at the club."

"I remember that drama well. She showed up unannounced at our front door in the city, asking to move in with Laura and me. That was a long night for all of us."

"My only other disappointment with her was her choosing Barnard over Stanford. I had some misguided fantasy that she would go to business school and join me in my company." Will's voice broke. "I'm so proud of her."

Bennie reached across the table and took his hand. "I am too. What are we going to do? I'm terribly afraid."

"Of course, so am I, but I think we should sign the Peace Corps application for her. Both of us."

"But your mother…"

"I'll handle my mother. I welcome the chance. I wonder how my life would have been different if I had insisted on going into battle." He held on to Bennie's hand. "And if I had refused to try and turn you into her idea of who you should be as my wife."

Bennie pulled her hand away. "I appreciate your saying that, but we've moved past how all this affected you and me. I'm sure you're not interested in listening to a recitation of how happy Laura and I are." Bennie remembered Will's sneering taunt when he found out about her affair with Alice. He had said, 'What do two women do in bed together anyway?'

Bennie began putting on her coat, and Will scrambled to help her with it. She gathered her purse and gloves. "What's important, and always has been, is Livie. Give me some time to consider what you've said about our signing for her. I'll call you tomorrow."

She ran down the steps and waved away the doorman's offer to whistle up a taxi. She crossed Fifth Avenue and turned north one block to the Pierre Hotel. The lobby was a jumble of ladders, tarpaulins, and paint cans. A group of construction workers were gathered around Laura. She wore a Chanel suit and held the jacket back with her hand at her waist. She saw Bennie standing in the door and rushed over.

"How was it? Here, let's go in here." She led Bennie behind the shrouded registration desk into what would be the manager's office.

"He wants us both to sign for her."

"Really! That will be over Olivia's dead body."

"Yes."

"So are you going to do it, sign for her?"

"Yes, I think we must. But I'm terrified."

Laura pulled Bennie into her arms and took her face in her hands. "We'll manage whatever happens. We always have." She softly brushed the back of her hand across Bennie's cheek. "Do you remember that frigid day on the campus at Mary Bradford School when I shared my fur coat with you? Before we went to see *South Pacific.* Before we started."

"Of course, I do."

"I fell in love with this face at that instant."

Their kiss was as strong as their years together and as certain as their future.

THE END

About Jane Alden

Jane, Donna, and sweet baby dog Lily live in Claremont, California, half an hour east of Los Angeles. California has been home since the late 1960s when Jane boarded her new little Ford Fairlane (with loan co-signed by her dad) and drove alone across the country to teach 7th-grade English in Porterville. After two years, craving bright lights and the big city, she moved to Los Angeles and began a thirty-year career in hospital management.

Across A Crowded Room, First Edition, was her first novel. She's working on her seventh.

Note to Readers

Thank you for reading a book from Desert Palm Press. We appreciate you as a reader and want to ensure you enjoy the reading process. We would like you to consider posting a review on your preferred media sites and/or your blog or website.

For more information on upcoming releases, author interviews, contests, giveaways and more, please sign up for our newsletter and visit us at Desert Palm Press: www.desertpalmpress.com and "Like" us on Facebook: Desert Palm Press.

Bright Blessings

www.ingramcontent.com/pod-product-compliance
Lightning Source LLC
Chambersburg PA
CBHW070651100726
47907CB00007B/2168